W9-AGO-695

Also by Zilpha Keatley Snyder

BELOW THE ROOT
BLACK AND BLUE MAGIC
THE CHANGELING
THE EGYPT GAME
THE HEADLESS CUPID
SEASON OF PONIES
TODAY IS SATURDAY
THE TRUTH ABOUT STONE HOLLOW
THE VELVET ROOM
THE WITCHES OF WORM
EYES IN THE FISHBOWL
THE PRINCESS AND THE GIANTS

AND ALL BETWEEN

AND ALL BETWEEN

Zilpha Keatley Snyder

ILLUSTRATED BY

Alton Raible

Atheneum 1976 New York

Library of Congress Cataloging in Publication Data

Snyder, Zilpha Keatley. And all between.
Sequel to Below the root.
Summary: With forces working both for and against the reunion of the estranged Kindar and Erdlings, two youngsters, one from each group, employ their own powers to resolve the matter.
[1. Fantasy] I. Raible, Alton, II. Title.
PZ7.S68522Ah [Fic] 75-29315
ISBN 0-689-30514-1

Published simultaneously in Canada by
McClelland & Stewart, Ltd.
Manufactured in the United States of America by
Halliday Lithograph Corporation
West Hanover, Massachusetts
First Edition

To All My Readers

AND ALL BETWEEN

CHAPTER ONE

There had not always been hunger in Erda. Even Teera, who was only eight years old, could remember when food had been, if not plentiful, at least sufficient to keep the stomachs of Erdling children from crying out so continuously that they were unable to sleep. It was no longer so.

Lying in her warm cocoon of furs, staring into the darkness, Teera listened to the cries of her stomach, and waited for the time of awakening when the fires would be fed and there would be a small food-taking of pan-fruit and rootbread. As she waited, she thought long thoughts about many things, but first and last and most often she thought of food.

It was most helpful to think of pleasant happy things, things that might distract her mind and help the time to pass swiftly. Remembering, imaging vividly, she relived good times spent with her favorite clan-siblings, Charn and Raula. Unlike most Erdling children, Teera had no true brothers and sisters, but Raula and Charn were caverneclan and thus almost as close, since their families' nid-caves opened into the same cavern and shared living space and cooking fires with her own. There were many good memories to review of happy hours spent in games, in exploration, and in the exuberant romping and wrestling indulged in by all Erdling children—at least before the time of hunger.

Teera had loved the romping. Often, before hunger made Raula weak and listless and Charn touchy and irritable, there had been hours spent in wild rollicking chases around the cavern, tickling, teasing, hugging, pushing and pulling one another, while their parents watched laughing. Relaxing on their benches around the central fire, the adults of the cavernclan, tired from long hours of labor, nevertheless delighted in the high spirits of their offspring.

Those times, wild and warm and exciting, Teera had loved best of all, but there were other favorite things to think about in the long dark time of sleeping. She liked, too, to think of hours spent in the surface tunnels beneath the Kindar orchards, where the sun came down strong and warm through the grillwork of Root and turned skin warm and brown and tingly. And where, at any time, a great juicy pear, or nut, or even a pan-fruit, might drop down through the grillwork, into outstretched hands. Just to imagine it, to think of pan-fruit, rich and sweet and filling, flooded Teera's mouth with water, and for the dozenth time she counted ahead to her next orchard visit. Not that she would eat a whole pan-fruit if she were lucky enough to find one. To do so would be unthinkably greedy and selfish. She would, of course, turn it over to the food wardens to be fairly divided, as was all food in Erda, but first she would at least be able to hold and feel it. To hold it against her lips and breathe its rich, warm, tantalizing scent. But it would be many hours yet, a full day and a half, before she was scheduled to visit the orchards.

There had been a time, not many years before, when there had been no restrictions on time spent in the orchard passageways. In those days, before the increase in their numbers had forced the Erdlings to regulate and ration so many things, the orchard tunnels had been open to anyone at anytime. It had still been so when Teera's parents, Kanna and Herd Eld, were children. Teera sighed, envying her parents' their unregimented and well-nourished childhoods. It would have been wonderful to have lived in those days of freedom and plenty. Often, to pass the long empty hours, Teera imagined herself backwards through time into those days and even earlier ones.

Like every Erdling child, Teera knew the history of her people through song and story and legend. She knew the sad, dark songs of exile and the rich, warm tales of early ancestors who survived to build a subterranean society based on a closely shared experience of sorrow and hope. She could easily imagine what life had been like in Erda when the enormous caves and caverns and myriad tunnels had been shared by less than a thousand Erdlings, and before that by less than one hundred, and on back to the time, many generations ago, when the first twenty exiles had been banished, robbed of their heritage by the powerful Ol-zhaan leader known in Erda as Dolwissener.

And long before that, Teera knew, there had been no Erda, and all people were Kindar together in the beautiful forest world of Green-sky. Except, of course, even then there were the Ol-zhaan, who were not truly people at all, but wizards, men and women of unnatural Spirit-force and cruel inhuman power. And so it had been, until the legendary Dolwissener, becoming angry at a small group of his followers who dared to question his decrees, sent them down into the great empty caves and caverns beneath the forest floor. Then Dolwissener had summoned the great force of his evil powers and sent it into a native vine that grew in great abundance throughout the forest. And the vine had leaped and writhed, and its roots had crawled forth over the surface of the land in an enchanted and indestructible barrier.

The story of those first Erdlings and the evil wizard, Dolwissener, was the subject of many of the long mournful sagas, or song stories, which the Erdling workers sang as they went about their work in mine or craftcave. They sang sadly of the cold, fierce, strength of the woven Root, a cold so fierce that it shriveled metal and reduced fire to pale frozen ashes. They sang of the huge dark caverns of Erda where the light carefree nature of the imprisoned Kindar grew dark and heavy, and where anger and sorrow smouldered like the banked coals of an Erdling hearthfire. They sang, too, of what they had lost, of birds and flowers, of great green-lit spaces, and of the easy splendor of the glide from height to height. In song and story they mourned a beautiful and carefree life that only a very few among them had ever actually known and experienced. Those few, known in Erda as the Verban, were celebrated in even more mournful songs and lamentations.

Besides the Verban there were also a number of the citizens of Erda who had been born as Kindar, but who had come to Erda as infants with little or no memory of their former life. Born to Kindar families, high in the forest cities of Green-sky, these infants had fallen from a window or branchpath before they were old enough to wear a shuba and, thus, to glide. Landing on the forest floor where, although often only slightly injured, due to the gentle gravity of Green-sky, they were doomed.

Doomed either to death by starvation—or to rescue by the Erdlings and a life of exile below the Root. Only now and then, an Ol-zhaan searching party came in time and an infant was retrieved from where it lay wailing among the giant ferns of the forest floor. But more often the searchers came too late, or looked in entirely the wrong place, and the watching Erdlings were forced to try to entice the little one to an opening in the Root large enough for it to pass through—into a lifetime in the dark underworld of tunnel and cave.

But although there was a special sympathy extended to these Fallen, the greatest pity was for the Verban, who came to Erda as full grown men and women, banished from Green-sky by the wrath of the Ol-zhaan. These few, having incurred the anger or suspicion of the vindictive wizards who ruled Green-sky, had been put into a deep stupor and while in this state, transported through the barrier Root by means of magic power. Thus the Verban came into exile with full remembrance of all that they had lost, and for them the yearning for light and sky, so well known to all Erdlings, was surely much more intense and painful. So the Verban were greatly pitied in Erda, and Erdling children were taught to treat them with the same solemn respect shown to a bereaved family at a Ceremony of Weeping.

Teera had known only a few Verban and only one well, a woman known as Lunaa D'ohn, who served as a teacher at the lower academy where Teera was still at the first level. Teera's father, Herd Eld, said that so many of the Verban served as teachers in Erda because the schools of the Kindar were much better than Erdling schools. Having been educated in the highly organized and efficient Gardens, the Verban were very advanced in such skills as reading and writing and memorizing. They were, therefore, very helpful in Erda schools, where a lack of books and a certain relaxed and informal approach to learning tended to result in a scarcity of graduates capable of even a rudimentary use of written language. Thus it was that Lunaa D'ohn, who had learned to form her letters on silk and grundleaf, taught Erdling children to make the same intricate shapes on slate and stone, and spent a great deal of her time answering their insatiable questions about Green-sky and the life of the Kindar. Teera, herself, although she knew that she shouldn't, asked the most questions of all.

In spite of the fact that she had been carefully admonished to respect the grief of the Verban and to refrain from asking questions that would remind her teacher of her loss, Teera's burning curiosity often overcame her scruples. And, truly, Lunaa D'ohn did not seem to mind. Speaking in her curiously crisp Kindar accent, she spoke of things that were endlessly fascinating to the cavern-born children. And Teera could have listened endlessly. Like the other children, she particularly loved to hear descriptions of Kindar food, rich and varied and abundant; but even more particularly, Teera yearned to know about gliding.

All her life Teera had desperately wanted to glide. She thought about it, dreamed about it, and quite often she pretended she could. Once, by transforming a lapan-skin cloak into makeshift wing-panels, and then jumping off a rocky ledge, she had managed to achieve a rather short glide with an abrupt and awkward landing. It had been an exhilarating and rather frightening experience, and Raula and Charn had both refused to try it.

"Play Kindar! Play Kindar!" Raula often said to her.

"That's all you ever want to do. Why can't we play rock-toss or chase-the-lapan for a change? The way you're always wanting to play about gliding and being a Kindar, a person would almost think you were a Verban, or at least a Fallen."

"I am a Kindar," Teera sometimes said, "or almost."

"I don't see why anyone would want to be a Kindar," Charn said, frowning. "They hate us. They call us Pash-shan and tell lies about us. They say we're monsters—beasts with long fur and claws."

"No, they don't hate us," Teera said. "They are afraid of us. Because of the Ol-zhaan. Because the Ol-zhaan tell them lies about what we're like. It's only the Ol-zhaan that hate us. The Kindar are kind and gentle and don't hate anybody. Lunaa D'ohn says so. She says the Kindar never hurt anything, not even animals. And my own grandmother—"

"We know," Raula interrupted. "Your grandmother was a Fallen. You've told us that a million times."

"Yes," Teera said dreamily, ignoring Raula's rudeness. "My own grandmother—a Kindar!" And holding out her arms and closing her eyes, she imaged the graceful fall of silken wing-panels. She could see them plainly, just as Lunaa D'ohn had described them.

Imaging, the production of vivid mental images, drawn from memory or borrowed from others, was a favorite pastime of Erdling children. All children were capable of producing remember-images, or summoning up vivid reproductions of scenes once experienced. And many were able to borrow-image, to share in the images of their peers by means of close contact of mind and body. And once Teera thought she had experienced a much rarer form of imaging. She had been certain that just once, she had time-imaged.

She had been playing with Raula and Charn, imaging in the usual way, when she suddenly became aware of a strange feeling of space and motion, and then a confusion of sensations that seemed unrelated to anything she could see or hear. The sensations sharpened and she, herself, seemed to become a part of them. It must have lasted for some time because when, at last she began to see and hear in the ordinary way, she became aware that Raula and Charn were standing close to her, their palms pressed against her face. Pensing the excitement and intensity of her experience, they had been trying to borrow-image, but apparently without success. Becoming impatient, Charn had, at last, begun to shake her.

"Stop it, Teera," he said. "Stop imaging. Let's play something."

"What was it, Teera?" Raula asked, her palms still pressed against Teera's cheeks. "What were you imaging?"

"I time-imaged," Teera had said eagerly. "I really did. I saw myself gliding. I saw that I really am going to do it someday, just like a Kindar."

Charn looked skeptical. "I'll bet you weren't really time-imaging," he said. "I'll bet you were just plain imaging. Only Gystigs believe in time-imaging anymore, and they believe that only very special people like old Vatar can do it. And even Vatar has to do all kinds of special rituals first."

"And fasting," Raula said. "My mother says that old Vatar fasts and meditates for a long time before he makes a prophecy."

"Well, I've been fasting," Teera said. "All there was left for food-taking this morning was a little piece of rootbread, and I gave most of mine to Haba." It was true, she was sure. Whether caused by simple hunger or something more mysterious, she had been feeling rather dreamy and light-headed for some time. "I did time-image," she insisted. "It was a fore-telling time trance, and it means that someday I will be a real Kindar and live high up in the forest." And spreading her arms, Teera had raced away, leaving Charn and Raula staring after her indignantly.

Remembering, Teera sighed, and snuggled deeper into the comfort of her nid. "It was real," she told herself, "and someday I am going to glide—high up through the highest branches of the grundtrees—and live in a beautiful nid-place woven of snow-white tendril and hung with beautiful draperies—and I'll eat and eat and eat."

Images of food, piles and stacks and tumbling heaps of food, were just beginning to soften into dream, when a voice intruded, and the lovely fruits and nuts and mushrooms faded away into darkness.

It was Kanna, Teera's mother. "Wake up, Teera," she was saying. "Your father is leaving soon for the Center, and he wants to speak to you before he goes."

Kanna was lighting the lamp in the alcove as she spoke, and her back was to Teera, but even without eye-touch, Teera could pense that her mother was greatly troubled. Teera pensed emotions almost without effort, as did many Erdlings, although the more advanced forms of pensing, such as receiving exact thoughts or words, did not exist in Erda. At this moment Teera knew without doubt that her mother was in distress, and that her sorrow was for Teera, herself.

"What is it?" she said slowly, not wanting to ask, because she was quite sure that she already knew. Her father wanted to talk to her about Haba. Teera knew because he had warned her only a few days before that there might come a time when Haba would have to be killed and eaten.

CHAPTER TWO

Haba was a graybrown lapan. Small, rounded, long-eared creatures, native to the forest floor, lapans had long been trapped by the Erdlings for their flesh and fur. Docile and easily tamed, they had in years past, also been kept by Erdling children as pets. But since the time of hunger, pets had become an unwarranted luxury. Haba, cuddly, playful Haba, whose soft warm fur was beautifully flecked with subtle shades of earth and leaf, was one of very few tame lapans left in all Erda.

As Kanna left the chamber, Teera sprang from her nid and, stumbling in her haste, half fell to the floor beside a small cage of woven copper wire. He was still there. Startled by her sudden appearance, he gazed up at her anxiously, his soft dark eyes showing white rims of fear. Then, reassured, he sat up on his hind legs, his nose twitching, and put his soft front paws on her fingers where they clutched the wires of his cage. As soon as the door was opened, just as he had always done, he jumped out into her outstretched arms. Holding him tightly, she buried her face in the warm fur.

"I'll never, never, never," she whispered fiercely into the warm softness. "I'd starve first. I'd starve a hundred times first."

"Teera," it was her father who spoke now, and looking up, Teera saw that he was standing in the doorway of her chamber. Shutting her Spirit to his pity and regret, she let her grief turn into anger.

"No!" she shouted. "No! I won't let you. You don't love me or you wouldn't let them. You could make them change their minds if you wanted to. I know you could. You just don't want to. You don't want to because you're—" She stopped, holding her breath, letting her anger build inside her like steam in a cooking pot, and then said something terrible. "—you're a wissener," she cried. "You are. You are. You're an awful wissener!"

But although she had called him by a term that meant heartless and unfeeling—one of the most insulting words she knew—her father failed to respond in kind, which made her more wildly angry than before. He should be angry at her for calling him such an awful name. He should shout back at her—justifying her anger and giving it fuel to feed on. Instead he was speaking to her gently.

"Teera. Teera. Lovechild. It's not of my doing. It was not my decision, and it would be wrong of me to try to change it. The food-warden spoke to me yesterday. The decision was made by the Council."

"But Oulaa Tarn still has her lapan," Teera cried. "I saw it yesterday. And no one has told her she can't keep him anymore."

"Yes," Herd said, "and for the time being she will be allowed to keep him. But Oulaa is crippled and cannot run and play with the other children. It is for that reason only that the Council has made an exception in her case. Just as Haba has for so long been an exception, because you have no true brothers and sisters."

A tall man, with dark deep-set eyes, Herd Eld, reached out with his arms and Spirit to his defiant daughter.

"You must not grudge poor Oulaa her lapan," he said. "She must wait alone in the cavern while my beautiful, strong Teera runs and plays—"

Wrenching her shoulders out of her father's grasp, Teera sank to her knees, closing her eyes and mind. Sheltering the soft warmth of her pet beneath her crouching body, she wailed with grief and anger. Sobbing and choking, she wailed louder and louder so that even her Spirit was deafened, and she could no longer pense her father's grief and pity.

Then Kanna was, again, in the doorway; there were voices, footsteps, and as Teera caught her breath for a louder wail, she heard her mother say, "Come away, Herd. Let her grieve alone. When she has wept awhile, she will see more clearly."

"I won't," Teera whispered. "I won't see." Rubbing her eyes fiercely with the back of her hand, she jumped to her feet, choking down her sobs. Quickly, she gathered up a few possessions—a lantern, a fur cape, a handful of favorite necklaces and bracelets. These she placed in a shoulder pack arranging them carefully so as to leave a comfortable resting place for Haba. Then, catching up her pet, she placed him carefully inside, tying the top flap down over his head. With the pouch in place on her shoulders, she tiptoed quietly to the door of her chamber, and down the narrow passageway that led to the cavern.

The sound of tense, anxious voices reached her ears as she crept silently past the beaten copper door-screen outside her parents' nid-cave. She hurried on without pausing until she reached the archway that led into the central cavern. There she stopped and peered out cautiously. The large cavern that served as kitchen and common room for four other families besides her own, was surprisingly empty. The many wall lamps were still dimmed for the time of sleeping, and dark shadows filled the far corners and hung low in the high arch of the ceiling. The stone tables and benches were still bare and clean, awaiting the hour of the morning food-taking. In the great shadowy expanse, only one figure moved. Near the central hearth Prelf Arnd, the father of Charn, knelt on the slate tiles, adding fresh coals to last night's embers. His back was towards Teera. Moving silently, she edged towards the cavern entrance and the tunnelway that led to the Center.

She would not actually go to the Center, the vast intersecting network of natural grottos and manmade caverns that housed the public buildings, exchanges, and assembly halls of Erda. But she would head in that direction because in the thickly converging tunnels of the central area, she would be able to change passageways and directions often, in case of pursuit. She would move then through the outlying areas and on southward towards the mines, the furnaces, and the huge smoke-stained manufacturing caves of the farthest regions.

Teera had chosen this direction partly because she felt sure that her parents would not expect her to choose it. Instead, they would look first in the direction that she had, at first, planned to go—to the northeast, towards the higher regions, which underlay the Kindar orchards. There, in the favorite playground of Erda children, in the warm sunlight where it might always be possible to find fallen fruits or nuts, one would surely look first for a runaway child.

So Teera went south, towards the industrial region, choosing a route that took her through only two of the smaller commerce caverns. She hurried through these quickly, passing between rows of small stone-walled shops, trimmed and decorated with grills and doors of beaten or engraved metals. Some of the shops were already open, but Teera did not stop to enjoy their displays as she usually did when she was leisurely wending her way towards the lower academy. Passing jewelry and toy shops without even glancing towards their intriguing wares, she hurried on until she reached the first factory caverns. There, where the public walkways wound past networks of smoke and ventilation tunnels, through noisy cluttered craftcaves, and along the sides of rail tunnels, she began to feel secure. In the smoke and confusion of the industrial caverns, it would be easy to avoid observation.

She walked for a long time, keeping mostly to supply tunnels, stopping now and then to peer into furnace caves where molten metal glowed in huge vats and steam rose in hissing clouds from the cooling pools. Or again into craftcaves where metal workers labored over intricately shaped tools or dishes.

At last the noise and stench of the factory caverns diminished, and she found herself wandering down a railway tunnel that, by its appearance, had long been abandoned. The iron rail was almost covered by loose dirt, and the walkway was rough and untended. After a while Teera came to a place where, just ahead of her, the tunnel seemed to disappear into darkness. From this point on, the overhead light jets were no longer supplied with fuel.

Hesitating for only a moment, Teera knelt down and unshouldered her pack. As she untied the flap, Haba's soft round face peered out, his nose wrinkling eagerly.

Lifting him out, she hugged and nuzzled him before putting him down to stretch his legs while she rumaged in the pack for her lantern. In his slow loping gait, the little creature began to explore the deserted tunnel, while Teera found her flint wheel, struck it, and lit the lantern. Haba had wandered several yards away, back in the direction from which they had come, but at Teera's soft whistle he returned obediently. With her pet back in the shoulder pack, Teera moved on down the abandoned tunnel.

Now that she no longer had to keep on the lookout for people who might see and remember her, Teera was free to watch for other things. Her plan was to look for air tunnels that were wide and gradual enough to climb. Although primarily dug for ventilation, many air tunnels were constructed at a shallow pitch so that it was possible to climb up them to the forest floor. Such tunnels were dug in places where the barrier of Root lay close to the surface. From the ends of such air shafts, it was possible to dig for roots and mushrooms, and even, by reaching out between the branches of root to pick sweet grasses, or set traps for plak and lapan. And it was from these vantage points in the areas that lay beneath the Kindar cities, that lookouts were posted to keep watch for fallen Kindar infants.

The first three tunnels that Teera climbed were profitless. Lying so close to the inhabited areas, they had obviously been visited often, and every root and mushroom had been harvested. Reaching out between the cold gnarled arms of Root, Teera found that even the grasses of the forest floor had been carefully plucked. Her groping fingers found only a few stubs of grass, which Haba swallowed greedily. At the end of the fourth fruitless climb, Teera decided to stop for a while to rest. The air shaft she had just climbed was particularly wide and shallow, and it ended in a sizable chamber. A nid-shaped indentation hollowed into the chamber floor and several alcoves such as might have been used for lanterns or supplies, indicated that it had once been used by a hunter or lookout. Overhead the Root wove in and out in a pattern that left several sizable openings through which came warmth and light and a fresh, clean fragrance. Extinguishing her lantern, Teera curled up in a small ball and with Haba cradled in her arms, she quickly fell asleep.

Some time later she awoke feeling sick and weak from hunger. She lit her lantern, replaced Haba in her pack, and then continued to sit, wondering if she would have the strength to get to her feet and go on. Now that it was too late, she thought of all the things she should have done. She should have tried to take some food from the cavern larder, or at least to have waited until after the morning food-taking, before she made her escape. Except that it might then have been too late. Perhaps by then her father would have already taken Haba away to the food-wardens. No, she had had to leave quickly. And now, she would die quickly of starvation, and someday searchers would find her bones with those of Haba, and then her father and mother, and even the wissener Councilors, would be sad for what they had done.

Tears rolled down Teera's cheeks and sank into the soft fur of her tunic. Her sobs became rhythmical, reminding her of a chant, the first chant in the Ceremony of Weeping. She began to sing a song, making up new words to go with the slow, sad music of the chant. The song was beautiful and very sad—about a poor, unfortunate girl and her beloved pet lapan and how they died a tragic death. The song went on and on, and without realizing how she had started, Teera found that she was going on, also. Somehow she had managed to get to her feet and make her way down the shaft of the air tunnel, and now she was once again moving southward along the half-buried railway.

That day, Teera wandered down many miles of deserted Erdling tunnels, and through long stretches of natural grottos and caverns. She climbed dozens of air shafts, to the place where each ended at the Root, and once or twice her climb was rewarded. She found two small tarbo roots, and once even a sizeable earth mushroom. She drank often from springs and rivulets that trickled from the grotto's walls, trying to ease the pain of her empty stomach by filling it with water. As the time passed, she stopped to rest more and more often, and at last, she again fell into a deep sleep.

She awoke some hours later, hungry and cold and very much afraid. Sitting in the cold darkness, she cuddled her pet in her arms and tried to bring back the fierce strength of her anger and grief. But it was gone. Deep inside where anger had throbbed and pulsed like the flames of a furnace, there now seemed to be nothing but cold, damp ashes. Under her hands the lapan's small round head was warm and soft, and he sniffed trustingly at Teera's caressing fingers; but her sadness for his fate was cold and stale, as she told him what she would have to do.

"We're going to have to go back, Haba," she said. "I can't find enough for us to eat, and its too lonely and I'm afraid. I'm sorry, but we must go back."

It was not until then that Teera, having decided to retrace her steps, began to realize just how difficult it would be. She had gone only a few yards back down the tunnel in which she had fallen asleep, when she came to an intersection and stopped, realizing that she could not remember which way she had come. She began to hurry, frantically plunging down one passageway after another, looking for familiar landmarks of any kind. But there was nothing, no outcropping of rock, no trickling stream, nor pile of fallen stone that seemed in any way familiar or recognizable. At last Teera's pace slackened and she began to cry.

Some time later, her eyes blinded by tears, she stumbled into the entrance of a large air tunnel. Wider than most, the tunnel led upward at an easy pitch and, drawn by the possibility that it might lead to a mushroom or tarbo root, Teera continued up it. The passageway ended in a small chamber so shallow that it was impossible to stand upright. On her knees, Teera reached out through the opening, an almost circular gap in the network of Root, and probed blindly in the soft earth of the forest floor. Her groping fingers encountered no root or mushroom, but there were several small clumps of grass. These she picked carefully. Although the grass was bitter and unsatisfying, she ate the first handful herself and dropped the rest into her shoulder pack, which soon brought the sound of eager nibbling. Stretching her arm as far as she could in every direction, Teera braved the gripping cold of the Root on her arm and shoulder and even on her cheek.

It was then, with her face close to the Root, that Teera realized that the gnarled branches of Root were cracked and withered and that the opening was larger than most. Withdrawing her arm, she removed her pack and placed it at her feet, and a moment later her head was through the opening and she was actually looking at the forest floor.

Excitedly, her fear and hunger momentarily forgotten, Teera turned from side to side, staring eagerly at every thing she could see. She could not, in fact, see very much, or for a very great distance. On all sides blocking her view of more distant vistas, large clumps of forest fern rose up and then arched downward. Beneath the arching fronds grew small bushes laden with great clusters of brilliant blossoms, and all around, just beyond her reach, were many patches of the broadleafed grasses that Haba most preferred. It occurred to Teera that although she could not reach the grasses, Haba could harvest them for himself.

A few minutes later, having put the lapan out through the opening, Teera watched her pet as he loped from place to place grazing eagerly on the patches of grass. For a few moments she was happy, delighted that Haba, at least, was satisfying his hunger, but it was not long before a terrible possibility occurred to her. Haba had always been unusually obedient for a lapan, and almost invariably returned to Teera at her whistled summons. However, he was obviously greatly excited by his new and strange surroundings and by the sudden abundance of food. Realizing that he might be reluctant to return to his confined and hungry existence, Teera had almost decided to call him back, when a chance happening brought disaster. Nosing into an unusually large clump of grass, Haba disturbed a nesting plak hen, who, shrieking with anger, began to beat him about the head with her stumpy flightless wings. In an instant Haba had disappeared from view, running in terror. Teera called for a long time without result before she began to cry.

"Please come back! Please come back, Haba," she sobbed. "I'll let you go again if you want me to, as soon as I find my way back. But I'm lost now and alone, and I need you. Please don't leave me all alone."

The deep green light of the forest floor faded slowly while Teera alternately cried and called, and it was almost dark when she suddenly realized that in her desperation she had pushed her way up until both her arms and even her shoulders were above the Root. Through the soft fur of her tunic she could feel the strange numbing cold of its touch spreading deep into her body. In panic she struggled frantically, first trying to pull her shoulders back through the opening and then attempting to force her way upward. She was still struggling sporadically, between fits of helpless sobbing, when the night rains began. Raindrops mingled with her tears and soaked through her long, thick hair. Her fur tunic grew wet and clammy. Suddenly, after one more convulsive spasm of almost hopeless struggle, Teera found herself free and lying at full length on the forest floor. She was above the Root.

CHAPTER THREE

When Teera's mother and father realized that she was neither in her chamber nor in the cavern commonroom, they were not immediately greatly concerned. It was to be expected that children, with their fresh, free strength of feeling, would not easily sacrifice treasures of Spirit and feeling to the cold hard necessities of reason. In assessing her feelings about Teera's behavior, the mother, Kanna, recognized that she was even a little proud. Annoyed, yes, at the necessity of searching for Teera before she could leave for her day of service, and still anguished over the Spirit pain that Teera must be suffering, but proud, too, of the depth and strength of Love that gave one so young and small the courage to defy parents and Council alike in the defense of a beloved pet.

The search began casually when Kanna and Herd set forth to visit the caverns of neighboring clans to ask if a small, rebellious girl child had, by any chance, taken refuge there. When it had been determined that Teera was not hiding in the chambers of any of her friends in neighboring clans, Kanna and Herd returned to their own cavern and considered what was to be done next.

Fortunately, it so happened that it was Herd's day to remain in the cavern watching over the clan's troupe of children, and therefore he was not expected at his place of service at the Council of Health. Kanna, however, was already overdue at the storage caves, where she served as an allocator of supplies of food and clothing to each of the many clans of Erda. So it was decided that Kanna should, for the time being, leave the search to Herd, and hasten on to the Center and the storage caves. Her bond-partner would then, after attending to the needs of the youngest children of the clan, go on with the search, leaving the cavern in charge of the eldest.

Thus it was that Teera's father was soon hurrying away from his home cavern in the direction of the orchard.

As he hastened along the ascending tunnels, Herd told himself that he would surely find Teera hiding in one of the passageways that underlay the huge orchards of the Kindar. These passageways, running as they did directly below the Root between each row of orchard trees, were of great importance to the Erdlings. Here where the giant grunds and rooftrees of the forest had been cleared away, and only the much smaller produce trees grew in wide straight rows, the hot, bright sun of Green-sky shone down unfiltered to the surface of the earth, and even below the surface, and into the Erdling tunnels, through the narrow gaps in the Root. Here, with only the network of enchanted Root between them and the sun and sky, those fortunate Erdlings scheduled to visit the orchard, lay naked on fur nids soaking up the vital sunlight, and watching for the occasional fruit or nut that might, in falling, roll down into the tunnel. Free from their daily duties, warmed by the sun and by the company of others in carefree orchard-mood, and always alert to the possibility of a sudden windfall of precious food, it was no wonder that all Erdlings looked on the orchard tunnels as a kind of paradise. And it was surely here that a child would flee who had decided to live outside the bonds of family and clan.

Herd was quite confident that, in spite of the fact that the gates to the orchard passageways were, in these days of hunger, watched by wardens, it would not be difficult for Teera to gain entrance. Wardens, like all Erdlings, were first of all human, and as humans they were given to lapses in the strict observation of duty. Once the incoming rush of Erdlings assigned to the orchard for the day was checked and admitted, it was much more pleasant to mingle, sharing the combined warmth of sun and communion, than to sit in lonely attention at the gates. Herd, on his own orchard days, had seen many of the wardens lounging among the crowd, chatting and sunning. It was quite likely that Teera had slipped past an untended gateway. And, since the scheduling was changed constantly, the others whom she encountered would not be aware that she was not a legal visitor.

When Herd reached the first orchard gateway, he had no difficulty gaining entry, himself. The warden, although still at his post, turned out to be an old friend, the father of a childhood playmate. After listening with great interest and sympathy to Herd's story, he allowed his friend to enter. But although Herd walked up and down every orchard tunnel, carefully scrutinizing every group of chatting, sunning Erdlings, he did not find Teera. He walked swiftly, greeting acquaintances briefly and stopping only long enough to ask if they had seen his daughter, Teera, but with no success. At last, he left the orchard and returned to the clancavern, tired and bewildered, and for the first time, tormented by twinges of fear for the safety of his only child.

The next morning, instead of reporting to their places of service both Kanna and Herd went very early to the chambers of the High Council off the great assembly cavern of the East Center. When the Councilors had begun to assemble, Kanna and Herd were admitted to the audience gallery of the chamber to await their turn before the High Council. As the proceedings of the day began, Kanna and Herd, in spite of their now growing anxiety, were intrigued to find that the person waiting with them to address the Council was none other than Hiro D'anhk, a Verban and a teacher and academician of great learning and wisdom. Neither Kanna nor Herd had met Hiro D'anhk before, although they had heard of him and had seen him from a distance. Indeed, all of Erda had heard of Hiro who, as a Kindar, had been a person of high rank and honor. Since his arrival in Erda, he had served as an instructor at the highest levels of the Academy and also worked on special projects of a scientific nature. He was today reporting on an attempt to provide the people of Erda with a means of limiting the number of their offspring.

Kanna and Herd listened intently as the tall, gracefully built man, whose dark eyes seemed almost hypnotic in their strange inner brilliance, spoke at length in his high, crisp Kindar voice. He was describing attempts that had been made in his laboratory to duplicate a drug that had long been in use in Green-sky, which, when consumed daily, prevented conception. In Green-sky, one essential ingredient was distilled from the mashed and fermented leaves of a parasitic shrub that grew only in the heights of the forest. The experimenters had, as yet, been unsuccessful in duplicating it.

Pensing her husband's intense interest, Kanna looked at him and smiled. Herd Eld worked as a Health Councilor, and as such had had to deal daily in recent years with illness that arose from hunger and malnutrition. And for many years he had spoken freely to all who would listen concerning the need to reduce the population of Erda, but with little effect. Not that he met with disagreemen or opposition to his views. It was simply that the warm and emotional Erdling temperament, along with their traditional admiration of children, made it hard for his counselees to remember and abide by the good advice of the Health Councilor, Herd Eld. Kanna's smile spoke of the many times she had heard her bond-partner speaking impassionedly concerning the need for something very much on the order of the drug that the tall Verban was describing.

When Hiro D'anhk came to the end of his report, Kanna and Herd were summoned to take their place before the Council. Herd spoke first, describing his daughter's reaction to the decision of the Council that her lapan must be turned over to the food-wardens, of her disappearance, and of the attempts that had already been made to find her. The men and women of the Council listened intently and, with the warm involvement typical of Erdlings, many of them were moved to smiles and tears—smiles for their appreciation of the beauty of the full, free emotions of childhood, and tears for the grief of the child, Teera.

Kanna spoke next, telling of their fear that Teera might be lost in the dangerous labyrinth of deserted mine tunnels, and also of her imaging that Teera was still alive.

"I imaged it strongly, only this morning," she told the Council. "I feel certain she is still alive."

"Are you then, still able to image clearly?" It was the Councilor, Traalya Harp, a large, big-boned woman with a kindly handsome face, who asked the question.

"No, Councilor, not often, and certainly not as children do, and this image was more felt than seen, but it came to me suddenly and strongly, as if I were trancing. I am not a Gystig, and I have small faith in such practices, but I have heard that spontaneous trancing does happen in rare cases, at times of great crisis."

Traalya Harp nodded in firm agreement. "I, too, have heard of such sudden and temporary gifts of Spirit, but I think they happen very rarely."

Then Kir Oblan, an elderly Councilor with a great mass of curly white hair, cleared his throat and began to speak, his sagging cheeks trembling with emotion. "I feel," he paused and swallowed with difficulty, "that it is wrong to bring such grief to a young child. Perhaps in this one instance we should—"

But at that point Herd, himself, interrupted. "No," he said, "we must recognize that we are in crisis throughout Erda, and there are steps that must be taken, however painful, to prevent the crisis from worsening. It has long been our greatest failing, as Erdlings, that we feel too much, too urgently, with no thought for tomorrow and with no—"

Kanna put her hand on her bond-partner's arm, and he paused, blushing at his own presumption. "We ask only," he said, "that the Council decree a free day for some of the workers in the mines and craftcaves, that they might aid us in our search."

The free day was quickly granted; the message went out to the criers; and the Elds, after offering their thanks to the Councilors, prepared to leave the chamber. It was not until then that they noticed that the Verban, Hiro D'anhk, was still standing at the back of the gallery, near the doorway. As the Elds approached, he stepped forward.

Extending both hands in the Kindar manner, Hiro D'anhk greeted them. His words were warm and kindly, and beneath the words the Elds were able to pense a deep involvement with their grief and anxiety. "I wish to offer you my sharing of your pain," he said. "I will release my assistants in the laboratory and my students at the Academy to join in the search of the tunnels. And I myself will search with them. I know what it is to wander alone in the tunnels of Erda." He paused, and the dark brilliance of his eyes seemed to focus inwardly, intensifying the pensing that passed between them, until they seemed to hear the words he next spoke with their Spirits as well as with their ears.

"And I, too, have known the loss of a beloved daughter," he said, and then he turned away quickly and disappeared through the double doors of the chamber entryway.

Thus it was that, by the second day of Teera's flight, hundreds of Erdling men and women were beginning to gather to search the many miles of charted and uncharted tunnels, and the forgotten or undiscovered caverns of Erda. But it was on that same evening that Teera in frantic pursuit of her runaway pet, became the first Erdling to stand above the Root and below the green and open sky.

CHAPTER FOUR

The sky was not green and bright, but dark and wet. Teera lay beneath the dome of a giant mushroom on damp spongy moss. Far, far above her seven moons of Greensky shone with gauzy brilliance, but swift-flowing rain clouds, roof-tree, grund, and Vine, shut out even the faintest ray of light. And yet it was a soft gray darkness, unlike the thick oblivion of the caverns. Huddling against the stem of the mushroom, Teera waited, dozing and waking, for the time of light to return.

She was damp and chill and very much afraid. Accustomed to the deep silences of the cavern, where almost all sound was man-made, she found the constant muted symphony of the forest floor mysterious and terrifying. Blending with the hushed whisper of the rain, were rustles and squeaks, distant cries and close intimate scurryings. Time and time again Teera tensed in panic, only to hear the encroaching noise die away into the underlying rhythm of the rain.

But just as the faintest tones of light began to dilute the darkness around her, a sound came closer than ever before, and suddenly something warm and wet and consolingly familiar pressed against her chest. It was Haba.

Hugging him tightly, Teera cried softly into his warm fur.

She slept then, briefly; and when she awoke, the forest was full of soft green light. Jumping to her feet, Teera stared in awed amazement. It was so bright and beautiful. The air moved and breathed, and colors seemed to swarm around her like bright flocks of birds. Dazzled, she drifted from place to place, looking, touching, smelling, transported for the moment beyond worry or fear or even hunger.

On every side were flowers and fern, soft green turf and spongy moss, raindrops glittering on leaf edges, brilliantly colored flying insects with long trailing wings, flocks of fat plak hens, small streams of diamond-clear water flowing over beds of jewellike pebbles. Everything everywhere dazzled Teera's eyes and mind. But most wonderful of all, most strange and new and exciting, was the air itself. Like the air of Erda, it could be breathed, and stirred by waving hands, but it seemed entirely unlike in every other way. After the still, earthy air of the caverns, forever tinged with smoke and the corrosive odors of burning coal and gas, the air of the forest was a miracle of light and motion. Warm and spicy and yet pure and clean, it seemed to live and breathe of itself, moving and glowing all around her. Moving with it, drifting from place to place, she kept putting out her hands to touch it and feel its freshness against her skin.

For quite a long time she did not think at all. Dazzled, mindless, like someone deep in trance, she had no thought of Erda, of her parents, sad and grieving for her by now, of the long dark stretches of tunnel between her and her home cavern, of the opening in the Root through which she had come and the need to remember her way back to it. She had, in fact, no thought even for herself, a child, hungry and alone in an alien world. It was as if the Teera of the past were gone, leaving only a bodiless phantom, composed of wonder and delight.

Hunger returned first, and slowly and reluctantly, Teera began to recognize the need to look for food. Releasing Haba to forage for himself, she began to dig in the soft earth and, before too long she had found several tarbo roots and some very small earth mushrooms.

With her hunger somewhat satisfied, she thought next of the opening in the Root through which she had come. She began to search for it, aimlessly at first, and then with greater diligence, but to no avail. As she searched, she felt more and more frightened; but when, at last, she sat down to rest, the fright faded. Even if she found the opening, she reasoned, it was quite possible she would not be able to force her way back through it. And even then, she would still be lost, with no assurance that she would be able to find her way to Erda. It might be better to search for Erda here, above the ground, where it was possible to find food. By watching for rising smoke it should be possible to find the part of the forest that overlay the city; and once there, it should not be hard to locate an Erdling lookout. The lookout could then be sent to tell her parents —and perhaps the Council, too. What would happen next, was, in truth, uncertain, but full of intriguing possibilities.

Teera pictured herself holding court at a tunnel mouth, while one by one, her parents and all the members of the Council, and perhaps, all her friends and acquaintances, climbed the tunnel to speak to her and offer comfort and advice. She pictured their amazement at finding her above the Root, and the many conferences that would be held to consider how to get her home to Erda. Surely there would

be a way. Surely the Council, in all its wisdom, would be able to solve the problem. And in the meantime, she could stay awhile above the Root. Her parents would know that she was alive and well, and Haba would not only be safe, but growing fat and sleek on the lush forest grass.

So Teera began to wander slowly through the forest looking for the column of smoke that would indicate an Erdling fire somewhere down below. From time to time she stopped to dig for roots or mushrooms and, now and then, she rested, lying on her back and staring up through vast glowing spaces to where grund and Vine formed an alien world, intriguing and terrifying.

Up there in beautiful, bright airy chambers, provided with wonderful things to eat, and with garments as soft and fine as the hair of newborn infants, lived the Kindar. And there Teera's own grandmother had been born, and had lived in green-lit splendor until, when still a toddler, she had fallen to the forest floor. From there she had been rescued and adopted into an Erdling family. Surely, Teera thought, the Kindar, too, would welcome and feed a lost and hungry Erdling child. The Kindar were, as all Erdlings knew, a happy gentle people, who sang and danced and never frowned or cried. A people who loved and honored children for their gifts of Spirit. Lunaa D'ohn, herself, had said that it was true.

Such thoughts occurred again and again to Teera as she lay on her back, staring upward, or as she wandered past large tangled masses of Vine-stem that looked as if they might be climbable. However, there were two things that kept her on the forest floor.

The first was, of course, the Ol-zhaan. Besides the kindly Kindar, the Ol-zhaan, also, lived in the high forest.

The powerful wizards, dressed in their shimmering white shubas adorned with seals of green and gold, lived apart, in a special grove full of temples and palaces. But they did not stay, always, in their temples. They went out daily to lead and teach the Kindar—to the orchards to see that the Kindar harvesters kept their eyes averted from the forest floor—and to the Gardens, where they taught Kindar children to hate and fear the dwellers below the Root, calling them Pash-shan and believing them to be monsters of inhuman shape and form.

The thought of the Ol-zhaan was enough, or almost enough, to keep Teera on the forest floor. But even if there had been no Ol-zhaan, there was, it seemed, another barrier between Teera and the world of the Kindar. This barrier she discovered in the afternoon of her first day above the Root.

Passing an extraordinarily thick and interwoven stand of Vine-stems, Teera decided to climb up it. Telling herself that she would not go far, at least not far enough to risk a meeting with an Ol-zhaan, she began her ascent. The Vine was full of loops and intersections that provided firm footholds, and for a few minutes she moved upward without difficulty. It was not until she decided to look back to see how far she had come, that the trouble began. Looking down, far down, to where the giant fern had shrunk and blended to a smooth green mossy carpet, she was suddenly overcome with a terrible meaningless panic. For the next few minutes, endlessly long and terrible minutes, she clung to the Vine in frozen fear.

Teera had no way to understand and adjust to the fear that gripped her, paralyzing her muscles and her mind. Born in a close, enclosed world, she had never experienced the fear of heights. This ancient inborn terror, relic of an ancestral world where all life moved in the grip of a much stronger and more deadly gravity, was unknown among the Kindar. They unlearned as tiny infants their inherited fear of falling. But to Teera who, at the age of eight, had never before experienced height, a dim ancestral voice spoke, telling her that she was about to die.

When, at last, she managed to unclasp her frozen fingers and move slowly and tremulously downward, she thought no more of climbing up to the world of the Kindar. And after a while she began to think more urgently of Erda and of her parents. But although she began to search more diligently, she saw no sign of smoke and found no tunnel openings. When night fell, she again slept beneath a mushroom with her lapan cradled in her arms.

During the second day, the wonders of the forest gradually lost their fascination. Not that it was less beautiful and inviting, but it seemed somehow, to have lost its power to distract Teera's mind from other needs and hungers. The food on the forest floor, roots and mushrooms, while fairly easy to find, was light and unsatisfying as a steady diet, and there were other hungers, too. The thought of family and friends and familiar places was once more becoming a constant gnawing pain, and her search for any clue to the whereabouts of Erda became more and more frantic. During the day she came across several tunnel mouths, dark holes between the tightly woven Root, but they were empty and deserted, and only empty echos answered her frantic shouts.

The day stretched on and on, and it was sometime during the long eternity of the afternoon that Haba once more disappeared. He had been foraging nearby not long before, but suddenly he was nowhere to be seen, and there was no response to Teera's calls and whistles. As time passed, her search became more and more frantic. Without the familiar presence of her pet, anxiety and depression were suddenly transformed into grief and terror. After stumbling aimlessly from place to place, crying and calling, she found herself at last, leaning against the trunk of an enormous grundtree. The trunk seemed endless, and Teera was suddenly overcome by its gigantic presence. Sinking to the ground, she cradled her head in her arms and pleaded inwardly for someone, anyone, to come to her aid.

She had been crouching there for sometime when she became aware of a thudding noise coming closer and closer. Leaping to her feet, she shrank back against the trunk, staring in the direction of the approaching sounds. Then, directly in front of her, the fern fronds were dashed aside and two figures bounded into the clearing.

Teera saw at once that they were men, young men, and that they were dressed in long flowing robes made of a fine and shimmering material. Their eyes were wide and staring, and Teera had returned their stares for several seconds before she realized, with dawning horror, that they both wore on their chests the dazzling green-gold seals of the Ol-zhaan.

CHAPTER FIVE

Teera gave herself up to die.

Only a few steps away the two Ol-zhaan stood motionless, slightly crouched as if ready to spring, their eyes dark and huge in their pale faces. There was no hope of escape, and nothing that Teera had ever heard gave her any reason to hope for mercy. But still, even as she cowered against the grundtrunk, in hopeless despairing panic, her sturdy Erdling Spirit had not surrendered itself completely. Against all reasonable expectation, it still asked to live.

An eternity of terror had crept past before one of the Ol-zhaan moved slightly. A gesture of hand and eye caught and held Teera's attention, and as she stared back into the dark eyes, she became aware that she was pensing—even through the blind barrier of fear she was receiving a message of comfort and good will.

The Ol-zhaan stepped closer and reaching out he grasped Teera's wrist; turning her hand palm upward, he pressed it to the palm of his own hand. At the touch of the Ol-zhaan's palm, the pensing became stronger and more unmistakable, and its message was surely of compassion and reassurance.

Then the other Ol-zhaan spoke. His voice was sharp

and sudden as were the voices of Verban, but entirely intelligible. "Can you pense her?" he said.

The first Ol-zhaan, the one who still held Teera's hand pressed to his own, and whose huge eyes seemed dark and deep as a bottomless cavern spring, nodded slowly without taking his eyes from Teera's.

"She can speak then?" the taller one asked.

"I don't know. I pensed feeling only—no words."

"You know what she is, don't you? She must be a slave child. A kidnapped Kindar. She must have been captive since she was a very young infant, poor thing."

Teera's fear, which had begun to subside, flared anew. That explained the goodwill of the Ol-zhaan with the deep eyes. He did not know what she was. He somehow did not know that she was an Erdling, to him a Pash-shan. He took her to be a Fallen, a child born to the Kindar, and that misconception undoubtedly caused his pity and goodwill. He surely would have killed her immediately if he had known the truth.

"But how is it that she is free now?" the smaller Ol-zhaan said, still holding Teera's eyes with his own. "How is it that she is above the Root?"

"I don't know. Unless it is true that the Root is withering, and there is someplace an opening large enough for a child of her size to pass through. What was it that you pensed?"

"Only that she fears us and begs not to be harmed."

Stepping closer, the tall Ol-zhaan said, "We must be very strange and frightening to her. She does not know what we are."

In spite of her fear, Teera felt almost indignant. Of course, she knew what they were. Did they think she was stupid. Swallowing the sobs that still swelled in her throat she managed to say, "Are you not Ol-zhaan?"

The two Ol-zhaan stared as if in great surprise.

"Yes, we are Ol-zhaan," the taller one said. "And are you not a Kindar child who has been held captive by the Pash-shan?" He put his hand on Teera's head, and she tried not to cringe beneath his touch as he went on. "You must not fear us. We are of your kind, and we would not harm you." Then speaking to the other Ol-zhaan he said, "How do you suppose she learned to speak. Unless some of the Fallen have been old enough to have learned speech and they have taught the others."

"Or else the Pash-shan speak as we do."

"I suppose that is possible. I can't remember being taught anything concerning their manner of speech. But I had always thought of them as being incapable of speaking as humans do."

This time Teera's indignation was almost great enough to make her forget her fear entirely. Her chin jutted, and she was on the verge of saying something terribly foolish, when she forgot fear and anger alike in a sudden rush of joy. Bounding across the clearing a small furry creature launched itself into her outstretched arms.

"Haba, Haba, Haba," she was whispering with passionate joy into the warm fur, when she realized that the younger Ol-zhaan was asking her a question.

"Is it yours?" he was asking. "What is it?"

"It's my lapan," she said. "His name is Haba. I lost him. I was looking for him."

"Haba." The Ol-zhaan stroked Haba's head gently. "And what is your name?" he asked.

"Teera. My name is Teera."

She would tell them her name, but nothing else, she thought. She had always heard that Ol-zhaan could see into your mind and Spirit as into a pool of clear water, and that nothing could be hidden from them. But these Ol-zhaan seemed to still believe that she was a Kindar and therefore not to be hated and killed. She could not imagine how she had been able to deceive them, but it seemed that she had. It occurred to her suddenly, that they seemed to be very young, hardly more than boys. Perhaps it was only the old Ol-zhaan who could steal your thoughts and words from the most secret parts of your mind. Whatever the reason, if they wanted to love and pity her as a Kindar instead of killing her as a Pash-shan, she was not going to be the one to tell them that they were mistaken. Glancing up, over Haba's head, through the screen of her eyelashes, she felt one corner of her mouth tip upward in a stealthy smile. But the Ol-zhaan were busy talking and did not seem to notice. They were discussing what to do with her.

"No," the younger one was saying. "And it would be wrong to take her with us into danger. I think we must take her to safety as quickly as we can and come back again later to search further."

"But it will be many days before there is another free time when we can get away and not be missed. And we have learned nothing yet."

"Perhaps we have." The youngest Ol-zhaan put his hand up before his mouth and spoke softly so that Teera heard only something about "telling"—about her telling them something.

A pang of fear thudded against her ribs as the older one answered. "That is true. You're right, Raamo. We will take her back with us, and when she is more accustomed to us we will question—" At that point he, also, put his hand before his mouth and lowered his voice to a whisper; and although Teera tried, she was not able to hear enough to understand his meaning.

"No," the one called Raamo said then. "She would be lonely and afraid. She must be with others who will treat her kindly and—I have it. I know where she can be taken."

She did not want to go with them. Even though she knew that they meant her no harm now, they might in the future. The little she had overheard of their whispered conversation seemed to indicate that they intended to take her somewhere where she could be more carefully and thoroughly questioned—perhaps by other older Ol-zhaan who could see everything in her mind. As the two Ol-zhaan took turns trying to lead her away from where she stood against the grundtrunk, she only shook her head, clutching her lapan and bracing her feet in the soft forest earth.

Then the younger Ol-zhaan, the one who was called Raamo sat down beside her and began to tell her about the place where she would be taken if she would go with them. It was, he told her, the home of his own family—his father and mother and a sister who was very close to Teera's age, and whom she would like very much.

"Are they Ol-zhaan, too, your family?" Teera asked.

"Oh no," Raamo said. "They are Kindar."

"Then how is it—" Teera paused pointing to the seal on Raamo's chest.

"One is not born an Ol-zhaan," he explained. "The Ol-zhaan are chosen—two each year from among the Kindar who have reached the age of thirteen years."

"And your family," Teera asked, "do they have all the pan-fruit they want to eat every day?"

Raamo nodded, smiling.

Shyly, Teera extended her hand palm upward. "Tell me," she said. "Like this."

"All the people of Green-sky have all the pan-fruit they want to eat," Raamo repeated, and with the bond of hand and eye Teera was able to pense clearly and strongly that no deceit lay silently beneath the spoken words.

"All right," she said, "I'll go with you," but before they had moved forward more than a few steps another thought occurred to her and she stopped again. "Can I take Haba?" she asked.

"Haba?" the taller Ol-zhaan said. "Oh, the little animal? Yes, of course, you can take him."

"They won't eat him, will they?" she asked.

"Eat him?" the tall Ol-zhaan stared at her strangely. "Eat an animal? Of course not."

But the mind of the tall Ol-zhaan was closed and dark, and Teera was not going to allow herself to be tricked. Turning to the other, she again asked for a pensed reassurance, and when it had been given to her satisfaction, she at last consented to accompany the two Ol-zhaan to wherever it was they intended to take her. It did not immediately occur to her that she would be asked to do what she had already attempted and failed—climb up into the heights of the forest by means of a makeshift ladder of Wissenvine.

It was not until much later, after a long trek down twisting forest pathways, that they came to a stop near a heavy stand of Vine and the two Ol-zhaan set about shaping the short green overgarment that Raamo wore into a carrying pouch for Haba. But when the pouch had been finished and Haba placed inside it, and when

Raamo then turned to the Vine and began to lightly and rapidly ascend it, realization dawned.

"No, no," Teera cried. "I cannot. I'm afraid. I will fall."

It was much later after many pleas and arguments on the part of the Ol-zhaan and many tears on Teera's part, that she at last consented to try. And it was much much later, after what seemed to be hours and hours of sheer panic, that Teera found herself, if not on solid ground, at least on a wide and solid surface. They had reached the first level of grundbranches and had somehow managed the perilous transfer from swaying Vine ladder, to the comparative safety of the branchpath. Once there, Teera, weak and shaky from the long ordeal, collapsed face downward. A few moments later she sat up and looked around with great interest.

The limb on which she was resting was quite level and wide enough to permit several people to walk along it side by side. To her right the branch gradually dwindled in breadth, and then divided into many clusters of smaller limbs. In places, these clusters joined with end clusters from another nearby grund to form dense thickets of twig and huge succulent grundleaves. In the other direction the branch grew even wider, dropped slightly, and at last, far in the distance disappeared into the huge solid wall of a grund trunk. All around, rising up from the earth far below in thickly twisted tangles, or draped gracefully over limbs and branches grew Wissenvine, the enchanted Vine that sprang upward from the barrier Root. Like all Erdlings, Teera was only too familiar with the cold hard strength of the Root, but it was only through the testimony of the Verban that the many uses of the Vine were known to the people of Erda. Teera had heard of the tendrils, which were supple and elastic when alive and growing, but hardened quickly to almost metallic strength when severed. She knew something of the many uses the Kindar made of the tendril, and she had heard too, of the Berry, whose sharp corroding sweetness brought to those who ate it a dreamy forgetful pleasure. Looking around her, Teera saw these things of which she had long heard for the first time. She saw everywhere long white fingers of tendril, and here and there, blood-red clusters of Berry. And directly above her head, a heavy strand of Vine bore a Wissenflower, its thick translucent petals pulsing and flaming with strange, deep shades of color.

Teera was on her feet turning slowly in a circle, staring avidly at the strange beauty of the high forest, when the sound of her own name brought her back to the reality of the present. Near her, the two young Ol-zhaan were seated on the branch in postures of total exhaustion. The older one, who was called Neric, was talking about the difficulty of the climb they had just completed—and the trouble Teera had caused them.

"Great Sorrow!" he was saying. "I almost wish we'd left her to the mercy of the Pash-shan. I'm exhausted."

"And I also," Raamo said. "But her fear is to be expected, I suppose. Openness and heights are as frightening to her as dark, airless tunnels would be to us. And perhaps, in the depth of her mind there is some memory of her fall to the forest floor. She was probably injured by the fall—and then to have been seized and pulled down into the earth by such fearful creatures—it is no wonder that the fear of falling causes her such great mind-pain."

"True," the other agreed. "There can be no doubt

that fear can cause great mind-pain, and other pains as well." As he spoke he touched his upper lip gingerly, and Teera noticed that it seemed to be swollen. "On the Vine," he said, "during one of her spasms of mind-pain, she kicked me full in the mouth."

They rose then, and taking Teera's hands they led her down the grundbranch, through the thicket of end branches and up the branch of the next grund. In a few moments, crouching in a thicket of branch ends the two Ol-zhaan peered out warily. Pushing her way in front of them, Teera, too, looked out from behind a curtain of grundleaf and saw a sight that filled her with intense excitement and a strange bittersweet longing that was almost like remembrance. Only a few yards away down a broad carefully cleared branchpath, a large airy structure seemed almost to hang in space beside the branchpath. Woven of frond and tendril, light and clean and spacious, Teera knew it to be a nid-place, the dwelling of a Kindar family.

CHAPTER SIX

Teera Eld sat on a balcony of the D'ok nid-place, singing softly and nibbling on a large slice of honey-dipped pan-fruit. The song went well with fruit and honey. Pomma had said that it was called the "Answer Song" and that it was very old, but it was new to Teera. She mouthed the words softly and sweetly, coating them with honey.

What is the answer?
When will it come?
When the day is danced and sung,
And night is sweet and softly swung,
And all between becomes among,
And they are we and old is young,
And earth is sky,
And all is one.
Then will the answer come,
Then will it come to be,
Then it will be.

Placing the plate of pan-fruit carefully to one side, Teera rose to her feet and began to dance in time to the rhythm of the song. She had only begun to learn the dance, but its intricate, irregular motions seemed to blend so perfectly with the rhythms of the song that it was very easy to remember. Teera danced softly and smoothly, enjoying the motion, and the swirl of the silken wing-panels of her shuba.

Teera was now dressed like a Kindar. Instead of tunic and leggings of lapan fur, she was wearing a shimmering silken sheath, with wide flowing side panels, attached by strong cuffs at wrists and ankles. It was a real shuba —the beautiful garment that made it possible to glide downward from limb to limb, and even to float briefly upwards on rising currents of air. But even with a shuba, a Kindar could not really fly—as Teera had once thought possible. Upward travel was accomplished by means of ramp and ladder—and high up, amid thick growths of small branches, by climbing from branch to branch.

All these things Teera had learned, not by direct experience, but by word of mouth. Since her arrival at the nid-place of the D'ok family, she had not been allowed travel of any sort. She had, in fact, been carefully kept within the walls of the dwelling place. Most of what she had learned concerning shubas and gliding, and songs and dances, as well as a great deal of other information about Kindar life, she had learned from Pomma, the daughter of the D'ok family and the sister of the Ol-zhaan who was known as Raamo.

Pausing in her dance, Teera looked through the open doorway into the nid-chamber, where at this moment Pomma lay asleep. Teera sighed and then returned to sit beside the plate of pan-fruit at the edge of the balcony. For many days now, Teera had lost track of the exact number, she had lived here, in the nid-chamber of Pomma D'ok, and had spent every waking moment in her company. At first, the waking moments had not been many, as Pomma seemed to require a great deal of sleep. This, Teera was told, was due to illness.

Pomma had, indeed, looked ill when Teera had first seen her. Teera remembered that first meeting vividly and in great detail. She remembered that when the young Ol-zhaan, D'ol Raamo, led her into the chamber, she had not, at first, realized that anyone else was there. Looking around, she had seen only that the room was large and airy, its wall panels woven in intricate patterns of graygreen frond and ivory tendril. Tapestries, heavy panels of richly embroidered cloth, were looped up with silken cords to permit the gentle warmth and soft green light of the forest to breathe through the chamber. Tables and chairs, of woven tendril sat here and there about the room, seeming, to one accustomed to furnishings of brass or stone, to be almost too delicately beautiful to be of any practical use. Teera had remained silently staring, transfixed with wonder, until Raamo spoke to her softly.

"You will stay here," he said. "With my sister."

"Your sister?" Teera had asked.

"There, in the nid," Raamo said, leading Teera towards a small alcove. There, hanging from the ceiling was a large hammock, a real Kindar nid, woven of living tendril. It was the first real nid that Teera had ever seen. Although the word "nid" had been retained in Erda—and was used to mean any resting place—it was only in the high forest of Green-sky that a true nid was possible—a living, growing cradle of pliable tendril.

As Teera came closer, she could see that the nid was lined and padded with silken comforters, and that among them, lying so lightly that she almost appeared to float, was a tiny figure. As Teera and D'ol Raamo approached, the figure stirred slightly, and suddenly two enormous blue-green eyes were staring into Teera's face.

She had been beautiful even then, when the wasting had stolen the color from her face and had left her skin as thin and transparent as the wing of a moth. The hands she lifted to Teera's in greeting were tiny and so delicate as to seem almost without substance. In a faint breathy voice she spoke to Teera, giving the Kindar greeting for a stranger, "Greetings, friend, and welcome." But as Raamo bent to lift her from the nid, Teera pensed grief so strongly that tears came to her own eyes in response. Although the faces of the brother and sister were bright with smiles, Teera knew that Raamo's smile concealed fear and grief.

But that had been days ago. Soon after, the two Ol-zhaan had gone away leaving Teera there with Pomma in the D'ok nid-place, and the memory of Raamo's grief along with griefs and painful memories of her own, had begun to fade from Teera's mind. There was so much to see and learn—and so very much to eat.

Everything was full of wonder. Teera had often dreamed of being a Kindar, but her dreams had been earthbound Erdling dreams, shadowed and enclosed by narrow horizons of earth and stone. And now, suddenly, there was endless light and space, dazzling colors and an endless progression of new experiences.

"Everything is so bright and clean," she told Pomma many times. "Everything shines with cleanness, even the people." Taking Pomma's thin hand with its pale translucent skin in her own sturdy brown fingers, Teera interlaced their fingers and smiled into the huge blue-green eyes.

And even on that first day, when she had been so near to dreaming the final dream, Pomma had smiled back at Teera. Even though she was weak with pain and the drowsy comfort of the Berry, her smile had echoed Teera's. And as the days passed, they had begun to echo each other in other ways.

Hearba D'ok, the mother, said that before Teera came, Pomma had for many days been unable to eat any solid food—except for the soothing Berry, which she craved almost constantly. But watching Teera eat, watching her gobble her first whole pan-fruit in months and months, watching her learn with delight the taste of honey and egg and tree mushrooms, watching her revel and glory in every food-taking, Pomma began to feel a faint echo of appreciation of the act of eating. She began to taste Teera's food in order to share her pleasure, and, very slowly, the pleasure began to be her own.

There had been many other things to share as well. While Pomma was yet too weak to leave her nid, she began to share with Teera the songs of Kindar children and, in return, Teera taught her the songs sung by the children of Erda. Many of the songs were similar, passed down from the days before the Root when all the people of Green-sky were Kindar together. But others, like the Answer Song, were new to Teera, just as the sadly throbbing chants of Erda were new and fascinating to Pomma.

Pomma loved the singing. Weak and sickly though she was, her fine, sweet voice rose and fell tirelessly, her face flushed and glowing, as if the music itself offered comfort and sustenance. Teera, too, enjoyed the singing, but she liked it just as much when they only talked together. For hours and hours she questioned

Pomma, satisfying at last her avid curiosity about the Kindar and life in the forests of Green-sky. They talked endlessly about everything and anything, but eventually every conversation returned to two favorite subjects—gliding and the Garden.

Teera had already known a little about the Gardens, where Kindar children spent their days, between the ages of two and thirteen years. Accustomed to the Academies of Erda, where one was taught a great deal about numbers and mathematics and a little about reading and writing, the curriculum of the Gardens seemed intriguingly exotic. Rather than classes in numbers and letter-carving, Kindar children attended Song and Story, and took courses in Love and Joy, and in the skills of the Spirit, such as grunspreking, pensing and kiniporting. It seemed to Teera that she would much prefer a Garden to an Academy—in spite of the fact that Kindar children were apparently required to spend a great deal more time at their place of learning than were the children of Erda.

Teera, like all Erdlings, knew of the Spirit skills, both from the Verban and from the old tales that their ancestors had brought to Erda at the time of the exile. She knew that at one time nearly all the people of Green-sky could pense, sending and receiving exact words and phrases by means of Spirit-force. She had heard also of grunspreking, the art of influencing and controlling plant life, and she knew that it had been by means of this skill, magnified to the level of enchantment, that D'ol Wissener had transformed the Root from a normal growth into a barrier of supernatural strength and power. She knew vaguely, too, of kiniporting, although she had heard but little concerning its history and the great significance it once had had in Green-sky.

"Why do they bother to teach it?" she asked Pomma. "Why is being able to make a leaf float through the air, or a cylinder roll towards you across a table, so important?"

"I guess it's not very important anymore," Pomma said. "No one can do it anymore except very young children, and they can only move things of very little weight. But it was very important once, because of uniforce. Do you know about uniforce?"

Teera had nodded uncertainly. "I think so," she had said. "I think in Erda it means great power—something like magic."

Pomma nodded. "It's like that. In the early days, before the waning of the Spirit, there were people who were able to combine their powers with those of other people, so that they were much stronger—hundreds of times stronger. It was by uniforce that groups of healers were able to end almost all sickness and the grunsprekers started the orchards. And uniforce worked with kiniporting, too. Most of the great temples and assembly halls were built by teams of kiniporters who were able to use uniforce to lift huge tree limbs and even the trunks of rooftrees and hold them in place for the builders. There are pictures of them, of the uniforce builders of Orbora, on tapestries all over Green-sky. And there are many songs and chants about them." Pomma sighed. "It would have been wonderful to have lived in the early days," she said.

"But people can still pense in Green-sky, can't they?" Teera asked.

"Well, the Ol-zhaan can, of course. And all little children still play Five-Pense. But most of them never reach the fifth level. When I was very small, I could do Signals and Choices, and then when I was five, for just a little while, I could do Images. But I haven't been able to pense at all for a long time now."

"Let's try it," Teera had said. "Show me how to play Five-Pense, Pomma."

"I can show you how it's done," Pomma had said. "But we won't be able to do it." And so, sitting cross-legged, facing one another, with palms joined, looking into each other's eyes, Teera and Pomma had pretended to play the sacred game of childhood. The game played by all children young enough to retain their inborn Spirit-gifts, and reverenced by Kindar of all ages as symbolic of the sacred nature of childhood, and as a vestige of the time when the gifts of the Spirit were common to all those who were born beneath the green sky.

Pomma showed Teera how, at the first level, a small bowl was placed upside down beside the players; one player then covered his eyes, while the other lifted the bowl and placed something beneath—or, at times, only pretended to. By pensing, a signal was given, telling whether the bowl was full or empty. And then there would be smiles and sometimes laughter, when the sending was truly received, clear and strong and accompanied by the deep sharp thrill of Spirit-touch.

Pomma had said they would only pretend, since they were much too old to Five-Pense, but almost at once Teera found that she could receive Pomma's signals, and it was not long before Pomma, too, was truly receiving. Teera had been delighted, but Pomma was almost beside herself with joyous excitement. It was not long before they had progressed to Choices and, very recently, they had begun to do Images; and there they had found a new fascination.

Through Teera's mind, Pomma found that she was able to see the tunnels and caverns of Erda, and through Pomma, Teera saw all the beauties of Green-sky—and even experienced, almost as if she were doing it herself, the glorious freedom of the glide. Pomma had shared with her the thrill of the first swooping fall from the branchpath, the long clean sweep of the glide through green-lit corridors of space, and the feeling of power and control when the slightest motion of arms and legs initiated a bank or turn or a soft easy drop to a landing.

"I know I could do it now," Teera told Pomma. "Now that I've imaged it. I know I wouldn't be afraid anymore. At least, not if you were there with me."

And Pomma's enthusiasm had echoed Teera's own. "I know you could," she agreed. "And just as soon as I'm strong enough and you don't have to be a secret anymore, we'll glide all over Orbora. And you'll glide just as well as if you learned at the Garden like everyone else."

Getting to her feet, Teera moved to the doorway where she could see into the alcove, but Pomma was still sleeping peacefully. It was mostly because of Pomma that the days had passed so quickly. And with the passing days Teera had grown more content and the fears and sorrows that had come with her to Green-sky had faded and diminished. It was only at night with the coming of darkness and the soft whispering voices of the night rain that Teera still, sometimes, lay awake and cried softly, her tears running down into the silken comforters that lined her gently swaying nid. She cried most often for her parents.

Although she had run from them in anger, she had

long since ceased to blame them for the edict that would have taken Haba from her. As her father would have said, she had behaved like a true Erdling—feeling and acting first, and thinking afterwards; and now that she had thought, it was too late. And so she cried, missing her mother and father and Raula and Charn and all the others she had loved and who surely mourned her now as dead.

But there were other times when she cried for fear. The Ol-zhaan D'ol Neric had come twice now alone, to do healing ceremonies for Pomma and to question Teera long and carefully. And although she knew, by pensing, that he still felt kindly towards her, she also knew that he still thought she was a Fallen. She knew also that he was still determined to find out more about her, and about all those who lived below the Root. Someday soon, Teera knew, he would find a way to discover her secret. Or, someday, he might take her away to see other, crueler Ol-zhaan, who could steal your thoughts from the very bottom of your mind. Til now, when he had questioned her, he had spoken mostly concerning things that she was able to discuss without betraying herself. She had answered carefully and slowly when his questions concerned such things as the food eaten in Erda, and the use of fire, and what smoke was and if it was dangerous. And so far, when he asked more threatening things, things about her family and about the appearance of those he called the Pash-shan, her tears had been enough to make him stop. But someday he might not stop. And then, too, there was always the possibility that Pomma might forget her promise and tell what she knew about Teera and the Pash-shan.

Of course Pomma knew. One cannot Five-Pense and

keep secrets, and besides, through imaging, Pomma had seen the caverns and caves of Erda, as well as the people who lived there. She had, at first, been terribly surprised and excited. When she fully understood the import of what she had learned—that there were no long-clawed monsters below the Root, but only people who looked almost exactly like Kindar and who called themselves Erdlings—her first reaction was to share her amazing news. She wanted to tell her mother, her father, anyone and everyone. She became so excited that Teera could not make her listen to reason—until, at last, Teera began to cry. Not gentle Kindar crying either, with only big liquid eyes and quivering lips, but good, loud, Erdling wails and sobs and flooding tears.

Pomma had stared at her in shocked amazement. "What is the matter? Don't do that, Teera. Don't be so—so awful." It was clear that Pomma was not just sorry for Teera's grief, but also embarrassed and horrified at her free expression of it.

"They'll kill me," Teera had wailed. "The Ol-zhaan will kill me if they find out. They always kill Pash-shan if they can. The only reason they haven't killed me already is that they think I am a Fallen. If you tell anyone at all, the Ol-zhaan will find out for sure, and they'll kill me."

But Pomma had never really believed her. She kept insisting that the Ol-zhaan would never kill anyone—or "dead" them, as Pomma always said, blushing. There was, Teera had discovered, no Kindar word for kill, and the use of dead as a verb to mean the same thing was considered highly indecent. But whatever it was called, Teera felt absolutely certain that the Ol-zhaan would do away with her very quickly if they knew who she really was. At last, Pomma agreed not to tell anyone, but she promised still protesting and obviously not convinced of the necessity, so that Teera was quite sure that it would take very little to make her forget her promise. So Pomma and her promise was one more thing to worry over, and sometimes to cry about while the soft forest darkness hid her tears and her sobs were muffled by the sound of the weeping rain.

Returning to her resting place at the edge of the balcony, Teera sighed and dipped another slice of pan-fruit into the saucer of honey, and the thought of dark, shadowy worries faded in the comfort of sweetness on the tongue. There was comfort, too, in the sight of Haba napping comfortably in the padded sleeping basket of Pomma's pet, the sima called Baya. The little creatures were cuddled together, and one of the sima's long thin arms was looped protectingly over the round body of the lapan. Teera sighed again, more happily, but at that moment the door hangings of Pomma's chamber were pushed aside and the mother, Hearba, entered.

She was carrying two lovely new shubas, a deep, soft red one for Teera and another of blending pinks and golds for Pomma.

Pomma, who had awakened at her mother's entrance, was still exclaiming delightedly over the new shubas—holding the red one up to Teera and saying how well it suited her, when Hearba interrupted.

"Put them on," she said. "Put the new shubas on quickly and then come out into the common room. It is time for D'ol Neric to return, and this time he will bring Raamo—D'ol Raamo, with him."

Pomma squealed with delight, and Teera, too, felt pleasure at the thought of once more seeing the young

Ol-zhaan whose deep feelings spoke to her as well and easily as any Erdling's. But her pleasure was mixed with fear because, although she had pensed him to be gentle and friendly, everything she had ever learned about Ol-zhaan told her that he should be feared and hated.

CHAPTER SEVEN

On the first day, the search for the missing daughter of Kanna and Herd Eld was a massive enterprise, involving more than half the population of Erda. Greatly moved by the sad plight of the Elds, the High Council had taken extreme measures, declaring a first-degree emergency, thus releasing all but the most essential workers from their duties, in order that they might take part in the search. Children had been lost before in the tunnels of Erda, and the Council had acted before to release workers to help in the search. But in most cases the emergency was given a much lower classification, and only selected teams from each industry or institution were sent out to take part. Herd Eld was, of course, grateful for the Council's response, although it soon became apparent that the reasons behind their decree, as well as its results, were not, perhaps, of the best.

Herd Eld, in his capacity of Health Councilor, was well known in Erda, and most of the members of the High Council knew him personally, or at least knew of him. His passionate advocacy of smaller families and a reduction in the population of Erda was well known to almost all Erdlings; and his advice was widely respected, if not often heeded. To the Erdlings, who were quite accustomed to leaders who spoke eloquently and passionately in support of noble standards that they were seldom able to maintain personally, Herd Eld's limitation of his own family to one small daughter seemed a sacrifice greatly to be admired. And that that one small daughter might now be lost to him, seemed a great injustice. Living, as they did, under the curse of the great injustice of their imprisonment, the Erdlings were highly sensitive to all injustices. Their response to even the smallest and most obscure, tended to be quick and unpremeditated.

During the first day of the search for the lost Teera, Kanna and Herd had reason to wish that, in this particular case, the Council had considered a bit longer and had been a little less generous in their response. The workers had been released so quickly and in such great numbers that adequate preparation and organization had been impossible, and the tunnels around the city were packed with searchers, crossing and recrossing the same areas, and occasionally stopping to ask each other exactly whom it was they had been sent to rescue.

On the second day, at Herd's request, the decree was reclassified, and a smaller number reported for search duty. By now, experienced tunnel workers—miners and plak hunters—had been appointed as organizers, and teams were formed, areas allotted, and path markers issued, so the search became more orderly and much more effective. In teams of three or four, the searchers ranged far into the outlying tunnels and caverns, marking the paths carefully so that they themselves would not become lost in the vast labyrinth that surrounded the city of Erda.

Kanna and Herd, having asked to be assigned to the far reaches, were included in a team led by one of the most experienced tunnel-men in all Erda. Yagg Olf was an old man who had spent most of his life as a hunter of plak and lapan. Since the small creatures of the forest floor rarely entered the Erdling tunnels, it was necessary to set traps above the surface of the earth by reaching out through the Root. Tramping daily through the outlying tunnels, far from the well-hunted areas around Erda, he had set traps from the mouths of ventilation tunnels in areas long since abandoned, and had even dug new surface tunnels in unexplored or forgotten areas. During his lifetime he had, himself, rescued two Fallen infants, and had found and led to Erda three terrified, exhausted Verban, whom he had encountered wandering in the far reaches. Perhaps no one in all Erda was better acquainted with the vast underground wilderness that stretched out apparently endlessly below the Root. But even Yagg Olf's knowledge was limited and incomplete.

"No one can know the tunnels," he told Herd, "not all of them. For myself, I wouldn't try to know them all. It is not meant that they should be known."

"But I've heard that you have led expeditions of the Nekom Society to look for the end of the Root."

"Yes," Yagg said, "I led them. I told them that I knew it was useless—a waste of my time and theirs. But they had petitioned the Council for the right to make the expedition and had asked for me as their guide, and the Council had granted their requests. So I led them. But I told them what I thought. I told them that the Root could not be outdistanced any more than it could be cut or burned. The Root, I told them, is not matter but meaning, and meaning is infinite."

"Are you, then, a believer in the Gystig philosophy?" Kanna asked.

The Gystig faith, once widely held in Erda but now waning in influence, taught that Erdlings were born to the Root as punishment for their sins and the sins of their ancestors, and that humble acceptance of their fate would ensure rebirth to the high forest when their Erdling life was over. It seemed strange to Kanna that Yagg, who was obviously a simple and practical person, would be interested in mystical philosophies.

"You are right," Yagg said. "I am not a good Gystig. I do not attend their ceremonies or follow their ritual. And I observe the days of fasting only when my food ration is so small that I have no choice. But I was reared in a Gystig cavernclan, and in recent years I have begun to think that someday, when I leave the tunnels, I may return to the faith."

"I am surprised that the Nekom would accept a guide with Gystig leanings," Herd said.

Yagg shrugged. "They were not interested in my beliefs, but only in my knowledge of the far tunnels. And I served them well. We did not find what they were seeking, but at least I kept them out of the crevices and rockfalls.

Kanna's mind chilled with a sudden fright for Teera, which Yagg, for all his seeming bluntness, appeared to pense quickly. "I'm sorry," he said. "I did not mean to frighten you. There is little chance that your daughter has wandered far enough to reach the unexplored areas. And all such hazards are fenced off wherever they have been found and charted."

But although Kanna tried to accept Yagg's assurance,

she found herself thinking more and more often of the dark bottomless pits, the narrow crevices, and the caverns where the slightest vibration from a footfall, or even a shout, might bring tons of rock crashing down from the ceiling domes. Not only as she trudged through the endless tunnels, but also at night when she tried to sleep, she was haunted by images of Teera, walking alone and tiny under trembling rock masses, or wandering blindly towards hidden precipices. By the fourth day of the search, Kanna's hands had begun to tremble constantly and her legs were so weak that she was almost unable to keep up with the other members of her searching party.

On the fifth day, an open Council was held to determine whether the hunt should be continued. The Council was held in the huge central cavern, because all the searchers were expected to attend and, since it happened to fall on a free day, many others would undoubtedly be present. Diversions were scarce in Erda, and any open Council was looked upon as a source of entertainment and attended by many who had little or no involvement in the matter under discussion. The disappearance of Teera Eld was by now general knowledge, and the huge cavern was certain to be packed by sympathetic and curious onlookers.

Kanna and Herd arrived early and were seated on the central platform not far from the seats of the Councilors. The spectators began to gather soon afterwards, arriving, for the most part, singly or in groups of two or three. Now and then, however, a large number of people entered together and made their way to open areas where they could be seated as a group.

Sighing, Kanna pointed to one such group, which

entered noisily and was making its way down the central aisle. Stomping their feet in close cadence, they, from time to time, shouted slogans, which were largely unintelligible because of the echoing noises of the crowd, and waved long poles on which were mounted emblems that vaguely resembled the curved knives carried by hunters.

"Look," Kanna said. "It is the Nekom. We'll be lucky if the Councilors get around to discussing the search before the free day is over. See there is Axon Befal. If he is allowed to speak, we will be here forever."

"There are Hax-dok here also," Herd said. "They, too, will undoubtedly wish to speak."

"Why? Why?" Kanna said, her voice shaking. "Why would the Hax-dok or the Nekom be interested in the search for a lost child? What has Teera to do with their magic spells or their useless hatreds?"

"Nothing, Kanna," Herd said, pulling her to him to comfort her. "It is only that they miss no opportunity to get a large audience for their message. It's quite likely they will scarcely bother to pretend that they are here because of Teera."

Herd's prediction proved to be only too true. As soon as Kir Oblan had stated the purpose of the assembly and asked for suggestions or statements from those who had been engaged in the search, Axon Befal, a short, swarthy man with flashing dark eyes, rose to his feet and asked to be allowed to speak. When the Councilor suggested mildly that the leaders of search teams should be heard from first, at least twenty Nekom sprang up and began to shout protests. Immediately, Axon Befal leaped on to the platform and, to the cheers of his followers, began to address the crowd.

"Men and women of Erda," he shouted in a voice that seemed to be too large and impressive to have issued from his narrow chest, "we are gathered here to extend our sympathy and support to the family of a martyr to our holy cause. Yes, a martyr. A martyr because it was in protest against the deprivations that have been afflicted upon us by our ancient enemy that this child ran away into the tunnels and became one more tragic victim of the unjust persecutions to which all Erdlings are daily subjected."

Pausing only long enough to allow his followers' roar of angry approval to subside, Axon Befal's voice rose again, louder and more hysterical than before.

The organization known as the Nekom, of which Axon Befal was the acknowledged leader, was not officially recognized, nor were its beliefs and tenants widely held among the general population of Erda. But because of its forceful and noisy tactics, it constantly received a great deal of attention. The stated purpose of the Nekom was the return to Green-sky and the elimination of the Ol-zhaan. To this end the Nekom held meetings, laid plans, made preparations and practiced strategies, all of which, in the face of the indestructibility of the Root, as well as the great power of the Ol-zhaan, seemed to most Erdlings to be to little purpose. But to those among the Erdlings whose frustration with the privations of their lives had reached an almost unbearable intensity, the lack of realism in the goals of the Nekom seemed unimportant. It was enough for them to find, in the Nekom, the opportunity to express their feelings of hatred and revenge.

Axon Befal continued his harangue, to the wild enthusiasm of his followers, and the variously interested, indignant, or amused response of the rest of the large audience, until his voice began to falter under the strain. A rasping wheeze became rapidly more severe, and as his voice faded into a hoarse whisper, Axon Begal delivered a final accusation—that the Ol-zhaan, and the Ol-zhaan alone, were responsible for his failing voice—a symptom, no doubt, of a fatal illness brought on by a lifetime of exposure to the fumes of the furnaces of Erda.

When the leader of the Nekom was finally forced by his failing voice, to relinquish the platform, he was almost immediately replaced by another speaker whose voice was often heard throughout Erda. She was called Bruha, and she appeared on the speakers' platform so suddenly that not only the audience, but also the members of the council were left wondering exactly how her right to be there had been established.

She was tall for an Erdling and extremely thin. Her deep-set eyes, fixed and fiery with inner certainties, had a strangely mesmerizing effect on her fellow Erdlings, whose convictions tended to be more wavering. Stepping to the very edge of the platform, she raised her hands high above her head and for several minutes, stood perfectly still. Only her lips moved, silently, and the reflected fire of the surrounding torches leaped and flickered in her eyes.

In the huge assembly cavern, conversation trickled away into a silence that grew gradually more complete. At last Bruha spoke into a stillness that was like that of death. Her voice was thin and high and of a piercing intensity.

"I appear before you, fellow Erdlings, to bring a message from the departed Spirit of the lost child, Teera

Eld. The Spirit voice of Teera has spoken to me and has told me that it is only through the powers of the Hax-dok that the Root will be destroyed and the people of Erda will regain their freedom. The Spirit of Teera admonishes the people of Erda to join the Society of the Hax-dok and by taking part in their holy rituals, hasten the day when the withering of the Root will be complete and the Erdling will again be free."

For many minutes the voice of Bruha rose and fell in hypnotic rhythms, and her audience listened in entranced silence. They listened intently, although most of them had long been familiar with the claims of the Hax-dok and with the elaborate rituals and sacrificial offerings with which the group had been trying for generations to reverse the enchantment of the Root and cause it to return to its natural state. The Erdlings listened because they had no choice, and while they listened many of them believed, however briefly, in the magical promises of the Hax-dok. But as soon as Bruha relinquished the speakers' platform and the sharp thin flame of her presence was no longer before them, they returned their minds to other things.

It was not until then that Kir Oblan, as the presiding Councilor, was able to hear the suggestions of the leaders of the search and to begin the discussion of what should be done in the matter of the lost child. After hearing reports of carefully conducted explorations, which had covered all the known and charted areas around Erda, and had even in many cases, extended far out into the unknown regions, the Council came to the sad decision that the search should be abandoned. The parents of the child, Teera, would of course, be excused from their duties at their places of service for as long as they wished, and were free to continue to search alone for however long they felt they must. But all other searchers would be expected to return to their usual employment.

The business of the Council was completed, and the assembly was dismissed; but before they could depart, an old man dressed in a flowing robe of unadorned lapan skin, arose from his place in the crowd and began to speak.

"It is Vatar, the old man of the Gystig," people whispered, and those who had started to leave returned to their places.

"My beloved Erdlings," the old man was saying in a voice that, although quavering with age, was yet rich and full. "On this sad occasion, may we take but one moment to offer our loving sympathy to the bereaved parents of the lost child—"

"Yes, yes," the murmur of approval spread through the crowd and many turned toward the platform where Herd and Kanna still stood, their faces wet with tears.

"—and at the same time to make humble supplication to the all-knowing Spirit for forgiveness of our sins, and to grant us the grace to accept our fate in the certain knowledge that true freedom lies only in the Spirit, and that—"

But now as the quavering voice continued, there were many who ceased to listen. Some continued to focus their minds and Spirits on the Elds, sending them their pity and sympathy, but others turned away, frowning, and began to move away from their places toward the exits. But even those who walked away maintained, for the most part, a respectful silence, so that the old man, Vatar, was not interrupted. With closed eyes, his face and hands uplifted, he continued to speak while the vast cavern emptied, until at last only a scattered few remained. Those few continued to stand with bowed heads until Vatar ceased to speak and then, crowding around him for his blessing, they followed him from the cavern.

In the days that followed, Kanna and Herd continued to search the far regions, carrying on their backs heavy packs containing nid-furs, and food and lantern fuel, so that it would not be necessary for them to return to Erda often for food and rest. Marking their path carefully, they ranged far out into the unknown areas until, at last, Kanna sickened and they were forced to return.

Then with Kanna safe in the care of the clan, Herd returned to the search and tramped all alone, farther and farther into the unknown regions.

CHAPTER EIGHT

Perhaps it was partly the new shuba, a beautiful garment of shimmering blending pinks and golds, along with the excitement of seeing Raamo again, that gave Pomma such an extraordinary feeling of delighted anticipation. Seated in the large, luxuriously furnished common room of her family's nid-place, along with her parents, Valdo and Hearba D'ok, and her new friend and sister, Teera, Pomma could hardly keep from leaping up and dancing about the room. Her fingers twitched and tangled in her lap, and her feet moved involuntarily in little dancelike motions. She knew her parents were watching her, smiling delightedly, and now and then Pomma smiled back. It had been a long time, a very long time, since she had felt so wonderfully happy and alive and had taken such Joy from anything at all—except, of course, the Berry.

At the thought of the Berry, Pomma's hand moved involuntarily towards the pouch that she kept at her waist—but then it stopped. There were no Berries there. It had been several days since she had kept Berries handy in her belt-pouch so that they could be quickly eaten when the dark, empty, pain swept through her body.

But the pain had been less of late, and besides, Teera did not like her to eat so many Berries.

"Don't eat those things," Teera always said. "When you eat them, your Spirit goes back into yourself so that I can't pense you at all. If you eat them, we won't be able to image for a long time. And I want to image some more about gliding."

"But you can have some, too," Pomma had said, holding them out to Teera, fat ripe Berries, oozing with thick dark juice. "Eat some, and you won't mind about not imaging."

But Teera shook her head, shuddering. "I don't like them," she said. "They make me feel strange, like everything was dissolving and floating away from me."

And so, because of Teera, there were no Berries now in Pomma's belt-pouch. But there was the beautiful new shuba, and the fact that Raamo would be arriving at any moment.

And then suddenly the door hangings were flung aside, and Raamo was there, along with the tall young Ol-zhaan, D'ol Neric, and Pomma was running to meet them.

For several minutes all was joyous confusion, an intermingling of bodies, palms, cries of Joy and hastily sung greetings. When, at last, the greetings were complete, Raamo turned his full attention to Pomma, and she preened before him, holding out her arms and twirling on the tips of her toes.

"See how much better I am," she told him, "and Teera, too." It was not until then that Pomma, looking around her, noticed that Teera had retreated to stand partly hidden behind the hangings of the hallway door. Reluctantly she allowed Pomma to lead her forward.

"Look how much fatter Teera is. Teera loves to eat," Pomma said. Raamo bent down and offered his palms to Teera in greeting, while Pomma chattered on about what Teera ate and how much.

"It is not to be wondered at that Teera was hungry when she came to you," Raamo said, smiling at Pomma. "She had been wandering without anything to eat for two days when we found her."

"I know," Pomma said eagerly. "And before that too, she was hungry. Teera says that everyone is hungry below the Root."

There was a quick exchange of glances between Raamo and D'ol Neric as Pomma spoke. Watching them, Pomma failed to notice Teera until she felt a touch upon her arm and turned to see Teera staring at her with fear-widened eyes. Guessing quickly that Teera feared her mention of those who lived below the Root, Pomma quickly turned the talk to other matters. Knowing that Raamo would be interested and approving, she spoke of Teera's dislike of the Berry, and of the games and songs that they had taught each other. But when she boastingly mentioned that she and Teera were able to play Five-Pense all the way to the third level, Raamo laughed unbelievingly and accused her of exaggeration.

"No," Pomma told him emphatically. "I'm not overspeaking. We can truly. I thought I was too old, too, but Teera and I *can* pense each other. We can do Signals and Choices all the time, and sometimes we can do Images. We can't do Thoughts and Words yet, but I think we're going to. Isn't that wonderful?"

Before Raamo could answer Neric interrupted. Asking Pomma to come and talk to him, he told Raamo to take Teera into Pomma's room in order to speak privately with her. "Wouldn't you like to speak to Teera, D'ol Raamo?" he asked.

"Yes I would," Raamo said. "Teera would you come with me?"

As Raamo started to lead Teera from the room, D'ol Neric lifted Pomma up beside him on the pan-wood bench and gave her his full attention. Thrilled and more than a little awed by her proximity to the young Healing Ol-zhaan, Pomma was momentarily speechless. Glancing down nervously at her fingers fidgeting with the edges of a wing-panel and then up at the faces of her parents who were watching from across the room, Pomma avoided the eyes of D'ol Neric as he began to question her gently. But before she could answer, there was a sound from the front entry hall, and Pomma looked up in time to see the door hangings thrown back as a tall young woman appeared in the opening. It was D'ol Genaa.

The beautiful young Ol-zhaan, D'ol Genaa, was well known to the D'ok family as she was, like Raamo, a novice Ol-zhaan and had been Raamo's fellow Chosen the year before. During the previous year she had appeared with Raamo at the many celebrations of the choosing and had gone with him on the Journeys of Honor to the outlying cities of Green-sky. As it was traditional for the families of the Chosen to accompany them on these pilgrimages, Pomma and her family had had many opportunities to observe the beautiful young girl Genaa D'anhk, who was now the Ol-zhaan, D'ol Genaa. But Pomma had never seen her look as she did now.

Tall and commanding and yet delicately graceful in every line and movement, D'ol Genaa stood framed in the arch of the doorway, her beauty glowing as richly as a paraso bird caught in a ray of sunlight. But there was something in the rigid contours of her face and in the dark intensity of her stare that made Pomma shrink back behind D'ol Neric.

"I, too, would like to speak to Teera," D'ol Genaa said, and as Pomma and her parents and even D'ol Neric stared in speechless surprise she swept across the room to where Raamo and Teera had paused in the door to the hallway.

As Teera disappeared down the hallway between Raamo and D'ol Genaa, Pomma stared after her uneasily. Hastily she tried to center her Spirit-force—to try to reach out to Teera in mind-touch, but without success. Teera had disappeared from view, leaving behind her only a faint wisp of feeling. It was only the vaguest and most uncertain of contacts, but Pomma recognized the answering tremor in her own mind as one of fear.

But D'ol Neric was speaking to her again, and she was forced to turn her mind to him. He was asking about the game of Five-Pense, and if she and Teera could truly play it together.

"Are you sure you are really pensing?" D'ol Neric was asking. "It's very good that you are trying—but Raamo tells me, you have not been able to pense at all for more than two years, and Teera cannot, apparently, send anything beyond essences and emotions. Raamo has been able to receive no more than that from her, and, as you know, his Spirit-force is very exceptional."

"But we can, D'ol Neric, truly. I have shown Teera all of Orbora by imaging, and she has shown me—" Pomma stopped abruptly, staring at D'ol Neric in consternation.

"And Teera has shown you what, Pomma? What has Teera imaged for you?"

But at that moment Pomma's father approached and began to address the Ol-zhaan, D'ol Neric. He was speaking about the great improvement in Pomma's health since that last ritual of healing, which D'ol Neric had performed for her, and of the gratitude and great Joy that he and his bond-partner, Hearba, felt. Never one to waste an opportunity for spoken communion, Valdo had, at that moment, great reason to find words of appropriate quality and quantity, and he was more than equal to the occasion. As the words of her father rolled grandly on, Pomma's mind turned again to what might be happening in the nid-chamber where D'ol Genaa had taken Teera. At last, taking advantage of the fact that D'ol Neric's attention was still being held by Valdo's speech, she slipped down from the bench and ran from the room.

Even before she reached the doorway to her nid-chamber, she heard the sound of Teera's sobbing. Unjoyfulness or—as Teera would have called it in her blunt-spoken Erdling way—anger, surged up in Pomma in a hot dark wave. Dashing into the room, she ran to Teera and put her arms around her protectively. Frowning sinfully, she stared at her brother and D'ol Genaa, mindless of the fact that they were Ol-zhaan and therefore deserving of the greatest respect and deference.

"Go away, Raamo," she said. "Go away and take her with you."

She turned her attention to the wildly sobbing Teera, and when she next looked about her, Raamo and D'ol Genaa had indeed gone. Alone with Teera, she caressed her soothingly.

"What happened, Teera?" she asked.

Breaking away from Pomma, Teera ran to her nid and threw herself into it, burying her face in the silken comforter. "That other one, that D'ol Genaa," Teera's voice choked with sobs and muffled by padded silk, was almost inaudible.

"D'ol Genaa?" Pomma asked. "What did she do to you?"

"Nothing," Teera wailed, lifting her tear-wet face. "Nothing yet, but she wants to. She wants to kill me."

"Kill you," Pomma gasped. "How do you know? Did she say so?"

"No, but I pensed it. I pensed that she is very angry. I've never pensed anyone so angry."

"But maybe it's not you she's angry at," Pomma said, and in her agitation she used the coarse Erdling words without shame or shock. "And she won't kill you. I've told you and told you that Ol-zhaan don't kill people. And even if she wanted to, Raamo wouldn't let her." But Teera's sobs continued until, at last, Pomma put both her hands over Teera's mouth and said, "Please, please, Teera, stop—doing that. Stop making that awful noise."

But even then Teera's wails did not abate, until Pomma said that the crying was bringing back the pain of her illness and that she would soon have to eat a whole handful of Berries, if it didn't stop. Teera quieted then and lay still, her breath coming in slow shuddering sighs. The shudders slowly diminished, the sighs became softer and more regular, and Pomma realized that Teera had fallen asleep. Picking up her pet, Baya, the lavender sima, who had been observing the whole scene wonderingly from the back of a chair, Pomma tiptoed out of the chamber and down the hall.

When she reached the doorway to the common room, Pomma stopped and peered carefully around the partly drawn door hangings. From this vantage point, she could see her brother Raamo engaged in conversation with D'ol Neric and D'ol Genaa. Except for the three young Ol-zhaan, the room was empty. D'ol Genaa was speaking, and her sharp clear voice carried easily to Pomma's hiding place.

"I'm sorry about frightening the child," D'ol Genaa was saying. "I see now that I acted too hastily. It is a fault of mine. It would have been much better to let Raamo speak to her alone. But if you will tell me what you have learned, I promise that—that I will not act hastily on what I learn. And as for betraying you—I do not know you well, D'ol Neric, but I know Raamo well enough to be certain that he would not be involved in anything evil. I will not betray a cause that Raamo believes in."

"Very well then." It was D'ol Neric speaking. "But for you to understand our purposes, we must go back to the beginning. To the beginning of the events that brought us here today. It began, for me at least, soon after the day of my Elevation to the ranks of the Ol-zhaan."

Shifting her position behind the heavy tapestries, Pomma was able to catch a glimpse of D'ol Neric's face. As he spoke, his lips were twisted by a kind of crooked smile that spoke of bitterness rather than of Joy.

"I came to the Temple thoroughly seduced and corrupted, as are all novice Ol-zhaan, by the fame and glory of the Year of Honor; but there is in my nature a strain of skeptical curiosity, and before long, questions began to arise in my mind concerning the life of the Ol-zhaan. I began to wonder why it was that the Kindar were taught that the Spirit-skills were strong and vigorous among the Ol-zhaan when, in fact, they are as rare among our holy colleagues as they are among any group of Kindar over the age of five years. It troubled me, also, when as a novice, I learned the true history of our race and of the terrible events that led to the destruction of our ancestral planet. I was troubled not so much by the knowledge of our past, as by the fact that the truth of it was kept from the Kindar. It seemed wrong to me that they should be kept in ignorance—that they were not trusted with the truth.

"And then one day quite by accident, I happened to overhear something that made clear to me the fact that my instincts had been right when they warned me that all was not well beneath the gentle sky of our beautiful planet."

D'ol Neric paused, and in the pause, Pomma heard the voice of D'ol Genaa asking, "And what exactly was it that you overheard, D'ol Neric?"

"I was exploring in the high reaches of the Temple Grove, and I had discovered a small suspended chamber well hidden in a heavy growth of Vine. While I was yet inside the chamber, I heard voices approaching and concealed myself behind a heavy fall of tapestries. A group of perhaps a dozen Ol-zhaan entered the chamber. They spoke together softly, and the hangings behind which I was hiding muffled their voices, but I was able to recognize the voice of D'ol Regle for certain, and that of the venerable priest of the Vine, D'ol Falla. I was able to hear enough to determine that I was present at a meeting of a select and secret group who called themselves the Geets-kel. This was a little over a year ago, shortly before you, D'ol Genaa, and Raamo were announced as Chosen, and these Geets-kel seemed greatly concerned about the possible choosing of Raamo. Most of them spoke against his choosing, but one—I recognized the voice as that of D'ol Falla—insisted that he must be chosen whatever the risk because of the need to make use of his unusual Spirit-force as a Vine-priest. D'ol Falla seemed to feel that Raamo's great gift of Spirit might be able to halt the withering of the Root."

"But what *risk* were they speaking of?" D'ol Genaa asked. "What risk would there be in the choosing of Raamo?"

"The danger that he might, by means of his ability to pense, discover some secret known only to the Geets-kel and kept even from the rest of the Ol-zhaan."

"A secret? What secret?"

"I am not certain. I could hear only occasional phrases, but enough to make it clear that these Geets-kel possessed some secret of such great importance that it threatened all life on Green-sky. Twice I clearly heard someone speak of an end to life as we know it. Of the exact nature of the secret itself, I could determine only that it in some way concerned the Pash-shan."

At the word Pash-shan, Genaa gave a sudden start and then, for a long time, sat very still. Neric was still talking, explaining how he waited impatiently all through Raamo's Year of Honor before he made himself known and asked Raamo's help in discovering more about the Geets-kel and their terrible secret.

"When D'ol Neric first came to me," Raamo said, "I did not know what to do. But then I decided that we should at least try to discover what it is that the Geets-kel know about the Pash-shan that is unknown to anyone else."

"But what could it be?" Genaa said. "What could

these Geets-kel know of the Pash-shan that is not known to the rest of the Ol-zhaan?"

Raamo shook his head. "We still do not know. Neric thinks that the Pash-shan, through the use of evil mind-force, may have gotten control of those who call themselves the Geets-kel—that they are somehow in league with one another. But perhaps it is only that the Geets-kel know that the rumors that speak of the withering of the Root are, indeed, true, and that the Pash-shan will soon be free to roam at will in Green-sky. Perhaps the Geets-kel have decided that if nothing can be done about it, it would be best to allow the Kindar to remain carefree and happy for as long as possible. But we, Neric and I, do not agree with such thinking. We feel that it would be best to let the truth be known, no matter how terrible."

"But the Fallen child, Teera. How is it that she is here, and how did she escape from the Pash-shan?"

"That, too, is a long story," Neric said. "Raamo and I decided to go ourselves to the forest floor to see if we might there discover any clues to the secret of the Pash-shan. We went secretly, of course, and without permission, during the afternoon of a free day. And while we were there on the forest floor, before we had time to make any other discoveries, we encountered the slave child and brought her here. But we do not know how she escaped, except that she spoke of forcing her way through an opening in the Root."

There was a silence before Neric continued. "And now, D'ol Genaa, we shall see if I was right when I once told Raamo that you would not sacrifice pride and power for any cause. Now that you know our secrets—and the full extent of our transgressions—will you join us, or the Geets-kel?"

"You do not know me as well as you think, D'ol Neric," Genaa said. "There is a cause for which I would sacrifice pride and power and much else besides. And that cause is the freeing of Green-sky from the curse of the Pash-shan. If you are correct in thinking that the Geets-kel are in some way in league with the Pash-shan, then my cause and yours are one. I will gladly work with you to uncover the secret of the Geets-kel."

Behind the door hangings Pomma stirred uneasily. Puzzled and troubled by what she had overheard, she suddenly felt greatly in need of comfort and reassurance. Abandoning her vantage point along with all effort to make sense out of what she had overheard, she entered the common room and ran to Raamo, holding out her arms.

"Where is Teera?" her brother asked as she climbed into his lap.

"She is sleeping," Pomma said. "She cried for a long time, and then she went to sleep, so I came back here to you." As she spoke, she pressed her cheek against Raamo's chest, comforting herself with his presence.

For a time the three Ol-zhaan said little, and then for a while Pomma grew very sleepy so that she was only vaguely aware that Neric, apparently thinking her safely asleep, had begun to speak again of troubling things, of the Pash-shan, and of how Raamo had been pretending that his Spirit-force was waning so that the other Ol-zhaan would be less wary in his presence and, by forgetting to mind-block, allow him to pense their secrets. And of how he and Raamo planned to make other trips to the forest floor.

Closing her eyes more tightly, Pomma tried to close

her ears, and mind also, to the frightening things that D'ol Neric was saying. It was terrible to think that the Ol-zhaan were not what she had always thought them to be. That they were not—as she had been taught in the Garden—-the great and good guardians of Love and Joy and Peace. Turning her mind away from the confusion and bewilderment of unthinkable ideas, Pomma managed for a time to shut out the voices of the three Ol-zhaan, and to sink deeper into the comfort of her brother's arms.

But then, suddenly, she was once more aware of words and meanings. The voice was D'ol Genaa's, and although it was as softly pitched as a whisper, there was something about it that felt like screaming. In spite of herself, Pomma was forced to listen.

"I am certain," D'ol Genaa was saying, "that there will be a way to protect Green-sky from the Pash-shan. But I think you are right that we must first find a way to learn more about them. We must discover what it is that the Geets-kel know about them and much else besides. We know so little concerning them. We must learn the source of their power, and just what its limits are. We don't even know what they actually look like."

At that instant a startling idea occurred to Pomma, an idea that seemed, at the moment, to be an inspiration. If they knew, she thought, if D'ol Genaa knew that the Pash-shan are not long-fanged monsters at all, but only people almost exactly like the Kindar, she would have no reason to be so unjoyful about them.

Opening her eyes wide, Pomma sat up and said, "I know what the Pash-shan look like."

The reaction of the three Ol-zhaan was all that she had expected, and more. They stared at her, startled,

attentive and, it was easy to tell, very much impressed.

"Yes," she said nodding firmly. "I know. They look just like Teera. I know they look like Teera, because Teera is a Pash-shan."

There was a moment, only a very brief moment, in which Pomma felt proud and pleased to be the one to tell such important and wonderful news. But then she began to understand that she had made a mistake, a terrible unforgivable mistake. She began to realize that even though D'ol Genaa no longer thought that the Pash-shan were monsters, her anger towards them was unchanged. There was no change at all in the harsh and bitter rage that lay like a great wound beneath the faultless beauty of the young Ol-zhaan's face.

CHAPTER NINE

The days that followed were, for Pomma, a time of changes. A time when hours of worry and mind-pain alternated with periods of great happiness. And a time when certain changes occurred that were completely unexpected—fantastic, mysterious, and more than a little frightening.

The periods of worry and mind-pain came, of course, from the knowledge that she had broken her promise, and by doing so had put Teera in danger. It helped a little to know that Teera knew what she had done, and understood why she had told the secret. But the worry was still great and troubling.

Of course, Pomma had told Teera immediately, and Teera had understood why it had seemed reasonable to think that D'ol Genaa's anger would go away as soon as she knew that the Pash-shan were human, and not monsters at all. That Genaa's anger continued, that she seemed determined to think ill of the Pash-shan—or Erdlings—was still a mystery to Pomma, and to Teera as well. They spoke often of it, and of other mysteries, in the days that followed, while they waited for the next free day when the three Ol-zhaan were to return. Teera, in particular, seemed fascinated, as well as terrified, by the beautiful young Ol-zhaan.

"She is so beautiful," Teera had said dreamily. It was the day after her frightening encounter with D'ol Genaa, and Teera was sitting on the floor caressing her pet, Haba, and talking with Pomma about the events of the previous day. "It seems strange that there can be so much anger and hatred in one so beautiful. In Erda people think it is shameful for the beautiful and fortunate to feel anger against the less fortunate. Aren't the Kindar taught that such anger is shameful?"

"I've told you," Pomma said. "All unjoyful feelings are shameful in Green-sky. There is not even a way to speak of such feelings, except to say you are unjoyful at someone—and even that is not really proper."

"Then why is it that D'ol Genaa feels so much anger toward the Pash-shan?"

"I don't know," Pomma said. "Except when D'ol Neric was speaking of why the first Erdlings were shut up below the Root, D'ol Genaa said that perhaps it was because they—deaded people," Pomma paused blushing, and then used the Erdling term—"that they had killed. And she said also that they stole children—the Fallen—and that they were flesh eaters."

Sighing, Teera gently pushed Haba off her lap and looked up at Pomma.

"Yes, I think so, too," Pomma said, and it was not until later that she realized that Teera had not spoken. It had not been with her ears that she had heard Teera saying that she thought D'ol Genaa had other reasons for hating the Pash-shan. But when she did realize what had happened and excitedly told Teera that she had pensed her words, Teera seemed uncertain about it.

"Are you sure I didn't say it out loud?" she asked. "I was thinking of saying it, so perhaps I did."

"No, I'm sure," Pomma said excitedly. "I'm almost positive I pensed it."

"My words?" Teera said uncertainly. "But Erdlings cannot pense words, or send them."

"Send something else," Pomma said. "Send something in words, and see if I can pense you."

So Teera tried. She tried for a long time, but nothing happened. At last she gave up, and they returned to spoken words to discuss the troubling things that were on their minds.

"Why do you suppose D'ol Raamo warned you so carefully to speak to no one concerning the things they were discussing?" Teera asked.

"I'm not sure," Pomma said. "Except, of course, he would not want anyone to know that they had gone to the forest floor, and that they plan to go again. No one goes to the forest floor except the Vine-priests. At the Garden our teachers tell us not to even look below—not to think of it."

"Yes," Teera said, "but when your brother spoke to us about being silent, he spoke most strongly about the importance of not mentioning that there are really no Pash-shan, only Erdlings, and also to say nothing about the Geets-kel. Tell me again, Pomma—what are the Geets-kel?"

Pomma shook her head slowly. "I'm not sure. I heard D'ol Neric speak of them when I was hiding in the doorway. He spoke of hearing them talking at a secret meeting. He said they were talking about—" Pomma stopped, contorting her face in an effort to remember. "He spoke so fast and I could not hear everything, but he said they mentioned Raamo—and a secret. He said the Geets-kel know a secret that no one else knows. The secret was about the Pash-shan, and it was very dangerous. I think that D'ol Neric and Raamo think that the Geets-kel are dangerous."

"But *who* are the Geets-kel?" Teera insisted.

"They are—" Pomma stopped again, reluctant to say what was on her mind since she had, for so long, been defending the Ol-zhaan to Teera, telling her that it was foolish to fear them.

"Ol-zhaan," said Teera nodding, and this time neither one of them noticed that Pomma had not spoken the word aloud.

But there were other times when they could not help but notice—other changes, unexpected and unexplainable. They happened suddenly, fleetingly, in the midst of games or conversation; and afterwards there was wonder, and some uncertainty, as to whether anything had really happened or if it had all been only a part of their playing. But more and more often in their games of Five-Pense there were times when they spoke—briefly—in exact words and phrases without voice or sound, and in other games, also, things had begun to happen.

Teera's interest in the lives of all Kindar children had inspired many games based on the practices of the Gardens. Taking the part of the instructor, Pomma had spent many hours teaching Teera the songs and stories and games and rituals used in the teaching at the Gardens. She had begun to teach Teera how to write with stylus on grundleaves, and with thread and needle on pages of silk, as well as many of the ritual exercises intended to prolong the skills of the Spirit, which were the birthright of every Kindar child. Together they had performed exercises that were meant to develop such inborn skills as pensing, grundspreking and kiniporting.

And Pomma also explained how those who had lost their Spirit powers were taught other skills, called illusions, which made it possible to conceal their loss, at least for a while.

When the changes began to happen, slight and fleeting and unpredictable at first, they were a source of excitement and mystery and sometimes almost of fear. The fear came not so much from the events themselves as from the way that they occurred, unexpectedly and for the most part uncontrollably. But the fear could not outweigh the strange fascination that grew stronger and stronger as the manifestations of growing Spirit-power became more frequent and less easy to ignore.

And there were other changes, too. With the improvement in her health and strength, Pomma was beginning to take a new and more active interest in many things. For many months, long before she had been confined to her nid-chamber by her illness, she had been sinking slowly and peacefully into a world of dreams, soothing, silent dreams, ever more deep and shadowed. Everything—shapes and colors, songs and voices, even thoughts and feelings—had become vague and distant and uncertain. And now, suddenly, everything seemed very near and bright and urgent. Each morning Pomma awoke with a kind of hungry eagerness, an impatient curiosity that made her scramble from her nid the moment her eyes opened, and which, at times, caused her to stand for long moments on her balcony gazing out into the green distances of the forest, and other distances of less tangible dimensions.

The days passed slowly and, at last, it was the morning of the day that Raamo and the two other young Ol-zhaan had promised that they would return to the

D'ok nid-place. From the moment she arose from her nid, Teera was unusually quiet, and during the morning food-taking she ate but little. It was obvious to Pomma that she was tense and nervous, troubled by the thought that she would again be questioned by D'ol Genaa. Pomma wanted to comfort her—reminding her that Raamo had promised to be present when Genaa questioned her—but there was little space for words at the D'ok table that morning. Valdo D'ok was in good spirits, looking forward to a special celebration to be held before the hour of high sun, in the guildhall of the orchard harvesters. He had been asked, as the father of a Chosen and therefore a personage of high honor, to give the blessing of the Berry before the ceremonial partaking. To insure that the blessing would be of appropriate length and phrasing, it seemed wise to offer several versions to his family for their advice and approval.

So while Pomma listened to her father's richly ornamented phrases, she tried to send a message of comfort to the troubled Teera. And when they returned, at last, to their chamber, Pomma said, "Raamo said he would be with you—that he wouldn't leave you alone with D'ol Genaa."

"Yes," Teera said. "I remember. And I thank you for your comfort." Her hands twisted tightly in her lap, and she looked around restlessly.

"Would you like to play a game?" Pomma asked. "It is more than an hour yet until the time Raamo said they would be here."

"I think I would like to embroider," Teera said. "It is still so difficult for me that when I try, it swallows all my thinking and keeps my mind from other things."

So the embroidery frames were brought out, and

Teera and Pomma absorbed themselves in the intricate and beautiful stitchery that was used by the Kindar not only to express their love of beauty and color, but also to record the written word. They were briefly interrupted by Valdo as he entered to hurriedly sing the parting, and a short time later by Hearba and her helper, Ciela, as they left on their way to the public pantries.

It was some time later that the silence of the nid-place was suddenly broken by the sound of footsteps. Pomma lifted her head from her work and stared at Teera. Teera's wide brown eyes were full of fright. The steps that were approaching were firm and swift and quite unlike the quick soft tread of Hearba's feet, or the more measured footfall of Valdo. Then the door hangings of Pomma's chamber were pushed aside, and D'ol Genaa entered—alone.

There was a long painful silence. A silence that throbbed with fear and tension. It was Pomma who spoke first. "Where—where is Raamo—D'ol Raamo and D'ol Neric?"

"They will be here shortly," D'ol Genaa said. "I had fewer duties this morning so I was able to leave the Temple a little early." As she spoke D'ol Genaa smiled, a perfect gleaming smile that illuminated her dark beauty with a light that dazzled, but left behind it no warmth or comfort.

"I would like to speak to Teera alone for a few moments," D'ol Genaa said. "Would you wait for us in the common room, Pomma?"

Pomma felt Teera's hand on her arm, and she did not need to turn to see the silent plea that she knew would be in Teera's eyes. "If you please, D'ol Genaa," she faltered, "I would rather—I think Teera would rather—

Teera could answer much better if I stayed with her."

The dark eyes turned swiftly, and Pomma felt herself flinch before them. And when the Ol-zhaan took her gently but firmly by the arm, she allowed herself to be led from the chamber.

In the empty common room, Pomma stood for a moment, bewildered—unsure just how or why she had let herself be taken away from Teera. Then she ran to the entryway and looked out. Frantically she looked up and down the wide branchpath, desperately hoping for the arrival of Raamo and D'ol Neric. But although there were several people on the path, they were all dressed in the brightly colored shubas of the Kindar, and even in the far distance, Pomma could catch no glimpse of the shimmering white worn by the Ol-zhaan. A group of chattering children passed slowly, off on some free-day expedition, perhaps into the open forest to search for trencher beaks, but there was still no sign of Raamo and D'ol Neric. At last she whirled and ran headlong across the common room and halfway down the hallway, before she came to a sudden stop.

Only a few feet from the door to her chamber, she stood, poised on tiptoe, swaying forward as she urged herself to go on through the doorway, and then backward as she pictured the dark command in the eyes of D'ol Genaa. At last, she only crept forward until she was standing just outside the doorway, still concealed from view by the heavy tapestries that draped the entrance.

A voice was speaking, but too softly for Pomma to make out the words, but it gasped and trembled and at times became choked with sobs. Then another voice spoke, soft but urgent. A pause—and a gasp, sharp and shocking—and a babble of wild frantic exclamations.

Tormented by indecision, Pomma put her hands over her ears to shut out the sound and spoke sternly to herself. "Go in," she said. "Go in to Teera. She needs you." But her Kindar training, ingrained, almost inborn, of respect and obedience to the Ol-zhaan was too great, and Pomma was still standing in the hallway when, a few minutes later, D'ol Genaa emerged from the nid-chamber leading Teera by the hand.

Teera's face was wet with tears, but she smiled brightly, and it seemed to Pomma that she was receiving from Teera a wildly confusing jumble of thoughts and emotions. Uncertainly Pomma trotted after D'ol Genaa and Teera as they made their way across the common room.

"Where are you going, D'ol Genaa?" she pleaded. "Where are you taking Teera?"

At the doorway D'ol Genaa finally stopped and, turning to Pomma she said, "You must stay here, and when the others come tell them that we have gone on ahead. Tell them that Teera and I have gone on ahead to the forest floor."

The heavy tapestries of the outer doorway fell behind them, and they disappeared from view before Pomma had time to wonder about a very strange thing that she was almost certain she had seen. Not only Teera's eyes, but the dark eyes of D'ol Genaa, had been wet with tears.

CHAPTER TEN

Darkness was spreading and the first fine fall of the night rains had begun before Teera returned to the D'ok nid-place. She had been gone for only a day, but for Pomma it had been the longest and most miserable day of her whole life. Her fear for Teera, mixed with her shame that she had done so little to help her, had grown more intense as each minute crept by.

It had been, perhaps, no more than half an hour after Teera and D'ol Genaa had gone that Raamo and D'ol Neric arrived. They appeared suddenly, obviously breathless and troubled, and they seemed even more worried when Pomma told them what had happened and how D'ol Genaa, too, had been crying when she and Teera left. The two Ol-zhaan left hastily, and Pomma was alone with her fears and worries.

Not long afterwards Hearba returned with Ciela, and Pomma had to hide her fears and pretend only disappointment that the Ol-zhaan guests had come early and had taken Teera away with them—to be questioned at the Temple. And if Hearba saw her daughter's wet lashes and sensed her despair, she undoubtedly thought only that Pomma grieved over her separation from her friend.

Pomma wished fervently that she could tell her mother all that had happened. It would have been comforting to share her fears and to receive Hearba's sympathy and reassurance. But it was impossible. There was so much that Hearba did not know and could not be told—about Teera, and the Pash-shan, and the terrible mystery of D'ol Genaa.

As the hours passed, Pomma walked anxiously to and fro in her nid-chamber, hurrying out onto the balcony from time to time to watch and listen. Several times she thought of asking her mother for a handful of Berries, but although the thought was sweet and tempting, she did not act upon it. It seemed wrong, somehow, that she should comfort herself with cloudy dreams while Teera was, perhaps, in great danger.

At last, as the soft green forest light slanted into twilight, Raamo returned, and with him came D'ol Genaa, D'ol Neric—and Teera—and quite suddenly everything was changed beyond imagining.

The moment they entered the common room, Teera and the three young Ol-zhaan, the change was apparent. Even the air around them seemed to be charged with high emotion; and all of them, and most particularly D'ol Genaa, seemed transformed. D'ol Genaa's dark eyes were drowned and dim, and her mouth was blurred by wavering smiles, and yet her beauty had never been so astonishing. She looked, Pomma thought, like someone lost in a joyful dream. And as for Teera—Pomma could pense her happiness with no effort at all.

The hour was late, and there was little time. Songs of greeting and parting were intermingled as the three Ol-zhaan hurriedly departed, leaving Teera behind them. Although Hearba and Valdo had been told that Teera had been taken to the Temple for questioning, Pomma could tell that they, too, were aware of something extraordinary, and were plainly very curious. When Pomma tried to hurry Teera away to their nid-chamber in order to question her, Hearba followed them. She busied herself about the room, lowering the night hangings across the latticed windows and fluffing the comforters on the nids. At last, turning to Teera she asked, "Did you enjoy your visit to the Temple, Teera?"

"I—I was told not to speak of—of the things I did today," Teera faltered.

Hearba laughed and lifted her hands, palms downward, in the Kindar gesture that asked for pardon. "Of course," she said. "And wise counsel, too, I am sure. The Ol-zhaan will know when it is time for you to speak freely. In the meantime, I beg pardon for having questioned you. But I will ask one more question. Have you eaten lately, or would you like a few morsels?"

Teera smiled delightedly. "I am very hungry, Hearba. I thank you greatly for your question."

So Hearba hurried away to the pantry, and at last Pomma was free to speak. "What happened? What happened?" she cried. "I was so frightened. I was so sorry I had not helped you more."

Teera threw her arms around Pomma. "Don't be troubled." She laughed. "There is no need. I could tell you why quickly, all at once, but I think I will tell you in the way it happened. Like a story."

Seated cross-legged, facing each other with palms joined, in the position of Five-Pense, Teera began her story, and the telling was not only by words, but also by images and shared emotions. "When D'ol Genaa began to question me," she said, "I was terribly frightened.

It seemed to me that her anger was blazing out like flames from an open furnace. I felt that she would become so angry she would kill me if I didn't speak, but I was so frightened that I could say nothing at all. But then, when she saw that I could not speak, she began to plead with me, and to tell me why she had to know about the Pash-shan. She began to speak of her father, who had been killed by the Pash-shan, and what a great man he had been and how much she had loved him. And then she said his name was Hiro D'anhk. And I said I knew a Verban in Erda whose name was Hiro D'anhk."

Teera paused, waiting for Pomma to realize the great significance of what she had just said. Then she went on. "D'ol Genaa didn't know what a Verban was, so I had to tell her all about them and how they are banished to Erda by the Ol-zhaan. But then D'ol Genaa said, 'But how? How can grown men and women pass through the Root?' and I told her that no one knows for sure, but most people think that the Ol-zhaan make the Root shrink away long enough for the Verban to be put through into Erda. And then she asked me all about Hiro D'anhk, and I told her what he looked like and how he was a very learned and honored man who taught in the highest classes at the Academy. And then we were both crying. And D'ol Genaa asked me if I would go with her to the forest floor to look for a way to get a message to her father. So I said I would, and I was so excited and happy to find out that it was not really Erdlings that D'ol Genaa hated, but only whoever had stolen her father, that I did not even remember that I would have to climb down the Vine again. I was afraid at first, on the Vine, but I remembered the imaging of gliding and the fear went away.

"When we got to the forest floor, we looked and looked for a tunnel opening; and when we finally found one, we began to call for someone to come to help us. But the first ones to come were D'ol Raamo and D'ol Neric, who had come looking for us and heard us calling. While we were explaining to them about D'ol Genaa's father being a Verban, Tocar came up the tunnel, and D'ol Genaa saw him."

"Tocar?" Pomma asked. "Who is Tocar?"

"Tocar is an Erdling who knows my father and who has been to our cavern, and he knew me, and he said that my parents had been—" Teera paused briefly and the happiness was gone from her face as she continued. "He said that they had looked for me for a long time and that they had set the time for a Ceremony of Weeping. But then—" Teera's smile returned. "—Tocar went away to get D'ol Genaa's father and to take a message to my parents to tell them I was still alive. We waited for a long time until finally Tocar came back with D'ol Genaa's father. They talked for a long time, and everyone was very happy. They decided that no one in Erda should be told yet about me, except for my parents, or about any of the things that they were planning. So Tocar promised he would say nothing—and then we came back here."

Pomma shook her head as if to set to rights the muddle that Teera's amazing story had made of her understanding. "But isn't D'ol Genaa unjoyful at the Erdlings anymore?" she asked at last. "Even if her father isn't dead as she thought, he *is* below the Root. Doesn't she think the Erdlings stole him?"

"No," Teera said. "She knows the Erdlings are not to

blame because her father told her so. And I told her that no Erdlings know of a place where a grown man can pass through the Root, because if they did, all of Erda would be free. It is only the Ol-zhaan that can make the Root grow and shrink away. But D'ol Raamo and D'ol Neric say it is not all the Ol-zhaan, only the Geets-kel, who put the Verban below the Root; the Geets-kel are the only ones who know how it is done."

"But what are they going to do about D'ol Genaa's father? How are they going to get him back to Green-sky?"

"I don't know, but I think they have a plan about how to do it, and how to get me back to my parents. They talked for a long time through the opening of the tunnel with Hiro D'anhk; but they sent me away to the other side of the clearing so I didn't hear much of what they were saying. I heard them say they were going to try to set all the Erdlings free from below the Root, but they are afraid of the Geets-kel. They made plans about what to do about the Geets-kel; that's what I couldn't hear. I could only pense that the plans troubled D'ol Raamo. D'ol Raamo was very troubled about what they were planning to do."

Teera's face puckered with concern as she spoke, but Pomma smiled confidently. "Raamo will know how to make everything come out all right," she said. "I know he will."

At that moment Hearba returned with a tray laden with fruits and nuts and pan-bread, and taking comfort in Pomma's words, and in the sight of the heaping dishes, Teera's joyful mood quickly returned. Soon afterwards, as the rain intensified and the moon moths' glow faded in their honey-baited cages, Pomma and Teera slept soundly in the soft springy comfort of their nids, and awoke the next morning in unusually high spirits.

After the long hours of fright and uncertainty of the previous day, there was great relief in returning to the secure comfort of a daily routine, a joyous relief that Teera, at least, found almost impossible to contain. Pushing, pulling and tickling, in what almost amounted to the rough and tumble romping of Erdling children, Teera made Pomma shriek and laugh with excitement. Watching the wildly romping children, Hearba and Valdo experienced delight in their daughter's renewed strength and vigor, as well as some parental concern—since they were well aware that it was their duty to discourage any form of play that might lead to harmful aggression. But the rough play continued to be good natured, and the morning food-taking came and went amid pranks and jokes and fits of giggling, before the adults of the household went about their accustomed duties.

It was near the hour of high sun, and Pomma and Teera were seated on the floor of the common room playing with their pets, Haba, and the sima, Baya, when, very suddenly there was the sound of strange voices in the entry way. A moment later three men strode into the chamber. Pomma recognized one of them as the Ol-zhaan D'ol Regle, but the others were Kindar and strangers.

Too startled and surprised to respond with proper courtesy, Pomma remained seated as the men approached, silently and purposefully. The Ol-zhaan gestured, and one of the men lifted Teera from the floor; and her fear was like a silent scream in Pomma's mind as she, too, was seized and carried from the room.

CHAPTER ELEVEN

On the night before, while Teera and Pomma had slept peacefully in their silk-lined nids, there were others in Green-sky who slept little or not at all. All over the city of Orbora, from the grand and luxurious nid-places on the lower branchways, to the smallest and simplest dwellings high up in the upper grund heights, the Kindar slept in placid reliance on the holiness and wisdom of the Ol-zhaan. And in the Temple Grove most of the Ol-zhaan slept too, secure in the tradition that set them apart behind barriers of honor and power. But in one of the most palatial dwellings of the grove, in a nid-place reached by a long covered rampway that led directly up from the central platform of the Temple grounds, the honey lamps shone long into the night. There, seated on a thronelike chair of ornately inlaid pan-wood, an elderly Ol-zhaan of stately build had remained awake and alert through most of the long hours of darkness. And when he at last arose, sighing heavily, he did not make his way to his nid-chamber, but instead only crossed the reception hall to a large padded settee. There, after carefully arranging a number of beautifully embroidered pillows, he stretched out his bulky frame in a manner that could hardly have provided great comfort to a person of such ample proportions.

The rains waned and the soft brightness of the seven moons shone briefly through the latticed windows of the palace, and then newly formed clouds again brought rain and darkness. Lying stiffly on the hard settee, D'ol Regle had stared as unseeingly in moonlight as in darkness, while he waited for the return of his messenger, and for the dawn of a day that would bring deeds unprecedented in the history of Green-sky. And while he waited, he laid his plans and thought back over the events that had made them not only necessary but inevitable.

Although he was no foreteller, D'ol Regle could almost have foretold, simply through his longstanding interest in history with its logical progression of causes and effects, that a disaster was in the offing. And he had certainly tried to warn everyone involved. Not only at the meetings of the Geets-kel, but also in the Council of Elders, and before the assemblies of all the Ol-zhaan of Orbora, he had spoken out against the choosing of the boy Raamo D'ok. He had even gone privately to the palace of the high priest of the Vine and tried to reason with D'ol Falla, herself. It was she who had insisted on bringing into the ranks of the Ol-zhaan, the strange child with his abnormally prolonged skills of the Spirit. But, as always, D'ol Falla had made light of him, and of his well-founded concern.

Actually, of course, it had all begun with D'ol Falla. And not just with her strange demand that the D'ok child should be a Chosen. It had begun perhaps, long before, when D'ol Falla, herself, had been chosen to join the Ol-zhaan.

Of course he had not known her then, since he was a few years younger than she, and was not yet an Ol-zhaan, but he had heard many stories of her early days in the Temple. Already, while she still lived among them, her fellow Ol-zhaan had made a legend of the tiny woman who, as high priest of the Vine, had for so long exerted so much influence throughout Green-sky. Stories were told of the early days of her novitiate when, so small and delicate that she appeared to be but a child, she astounded her fellow Ol-zhaan with her brilliance and her many skills and talents.

But to some it had always been apparent that, along with her undeniable accomplishments, she had also used her charm and beauty to gain quick and easy admittance into every stronghold of honor and power. In the old records of the Geets-kel it was recorded that D'ol Falla had been asked to join that most select group before she had reached the age of twenty years. D'ol Regle, himself, had been asked to join at an unusually early age since the rule had been to limit membership to those who had proven themselves true Ol-zhaan over a period of many years. But, still, he had been past thirty when he was initiated into the secrets of the Geets-kel.

There had been, of course, a reason why D'ol Falla had been accepted at such an early age. Even in those days, now so many years past, the Council of Elders had begun to fear that the waning of the Spirit-skills among the Ol-zhaan would threaten the Spirit-evoked qualities of the Wissenvine. Not that there had been, at that time, any noticeable withering or deterioration of the Root. But since all the supernatural qualities of the Vine—the strange intangible beauty of the Blossom, the soothing comfort of the Berry, and the invincible strength of the

Root—had been called forth by the Spirit-force of the great D'ol Wissen, there was concern that a lack of the Spirit-skill of grunspreking might, in time, allow those qualities to disappear. Even then, most of the recent novitiates had demonstrated no ability at all in grunspreking, or in any other of the Spirit-skills. Thus, when the brilliant new novice, D'ol Falla, was able to show that she still retained some degree of Spirit-power, the Council was eager to have her become not only one of the Vine-priests but the First among them.

If there had not been pressure to make D'ol Falla the high priest, she might not have become a Geets-kel at such an early age. There were priests of the Vine who were not Geets-kel, but they, of course, never accompanied those special processions that carried the drugged body of a banished Kindar to the opening in the Root. But since tradition demanded that the high priest accompany every procession to the forest floor, it had been essential, since the time of D'ol Wissen and the spreading of the Root, that the high priest of the Vine be also a member of the secret organization of the Geets-kel. So it was that when the Council—which in those days was not so completely controlled by members of the Geets-kel—elected the youthful D'ol Falla to the position of high priest of the Vine, it was also necessary that she be quickly initiated into the society whose duty it was to carry the burden of secret knowledge concerning the true nature of the Pash-shan.

The honor and power of the high priest of the Vine was a matter of ancient and holy tradition dating back to the first high priest, D'ol Wissen himself, the greatest and most powerful Ol-zhaan who had ever lived. There were, of course, some who might argue that D'ol

Nesh-om, the early teacher and Spirit-leader, was of as great importance. And it was true that D'ol Nesh-om, as the guide and teacher of the first generations of Kindar, had been a great force and influence in the early days of the planet. But as all Geets-kel knew, it had been D'ol Wissen who had prevailed in the great controversy concerning the protection of the innocence of the Kindar. And it was D'ol Wissen who, after the death of D'ol Nesh-om, evoked the protection of the holy Root and thereby made possible the continued peaceful security of all Green-sky under the protection of the Ol-zhaan.

D'ol Regle sighed, rearranging his cramped limbs with difficulty. It was ironic, he thought, that he, who had dedicated his life to the memory of the great Vine-priest, might never achieve his secret ambition to follow in the footsteps of his idol. He had never doubted that he had good reason for his high ambition. Had he not been the most avid promoter of celebrations and Free Days honoring the memory of the holy D'ol Wissen? And would it not be only just for him, D'ol Regle, the acknowledged authority on ancient history, to dwell in the ancient palace of the Vine-priest, with its access to the chamber of the Forgotten where lay all the ancient records and documents. And had he not felt, always, that it was somehow his true destiny to lead the holy processions. It seemed unfair, indeed, that he had been kept from that high honor by the existence of one individual. An individual of delicate and fragile stature, who seemed, however, to be endowed with amazingly tenacious good health and vigor.

But now it seemed that D'ol Falla's strange influence over her fellow Ol-zhaan had, at last, brought them, and all Green-sky, to the edge of disaster. She had had her way in the matter of the choosing of Raamo D'ok, in spite of the fact that she knew well the danger involved in bringing into their midst a novice who, through his abnormal skill in pensing, could easily discover secrets for which he was as yet unprepared. The results could be complete disaster; and might certainly be so, were it not for the good offices of the zealous and dutiful novice, D'ol Salaat.

Only a few hours before, soon after the first fall of rain, D'ol Salaat had come to him, breathless and in haste, and had told him an incredible story. A story of treachery and intrigue that involved not only D'ol Raamo, but two other youthful Ol-zhaan.

D'ol Salaat, it seemed, had grown suspicious of the strange behavior of two of his fellow novices, and had begun to follow them, secretly and from a safe distance. Thus engaged, he had, only the day before, followed them all the way to the forest floor. He had been well aware, of course, of the risks involved; but feeling, as he did, that his own future was of less importance than the need to expose such evil behavior, he had persevered. And once on the forest floor he had, from a distance, observed what must have been a meeting between three Ol-zhaan and the Pash-shan.

D'ol Salaat had identified the three Ol-zhaan whom he had followed as the two first year novices, D'ol Raamo and D'ol Genaa, along with another youthful Ol-zhaan, D'ol Neric, who had completed his novitiate less than two years before. With them had been a small female child, whom they had left at the nid-place of Raamo's family before they returned to the Temple Grove. D'ol Salaat had been able to observe the child at fairly close range, and he felt certain she was not the younger sister of D'ol Raamo, although she was apparently of about the same age. Who she was, and why the three rebels had taken her with them to the forest floor, was a mystery to D'ol Salaat, as it certainly was to D'ol Regle himself.

It had been immediately apparent that action would have to be taken. At the very least, such shocking disregard of the taboo against all things below, would have to be corrected. But there was, of course, a much greater issue involved. It seemed certain that the three renegades, as well as their mysterious girl child, were now in possession of dangerous knowledge—knowledge concerning the true nature of the Pash-shan, forbidden to all except the members of the Geets-kel.

After confirming by skillful questioning that D'ol Salaat had not himself seen the Pash-shan and harbored no dangerous suspicions, D'ol Regle had entrusted him with a new assignment. He had been sent back to the novice hall with instructions to keep watch and to again follow D'ol Raamo and D'ol Genaa when they next left their chambers.

So, as the long night wore on, D'ol Regle waited for the return of his lookout, and pondered the significance of what he had learned as well as what must be done about it. And in his pondering there was one fact to which he returned again and again, one bit of information which, although it was not yet conclusive, intrigued him more and more as the night wore on.

According to the novice D'ol Salaat, D'ol Regle had not been the only person to whom he had gone with his shocking story. He had taken his report first to the highest authority, as was right and natural. He had gone immediately to the palace of the Vine-priest and spoken to the ancient D'ol Falla, telling her in full detail everything that he had later told D'ol Regle.

"And what was her response?" D'ol Regle had questioned the novice.

"She told me to go home to my nid and get some rest, and that she would consider what was to be done."

"Did she tell you to come to me with your story?"

"No, it was afterwards on my way to the novice hall that it occurred to me that it might be well for me to speak to you also, D'ol Regle. I'm not sure why, except that it seemed to me that you had as much right to be informed of so serious a matter as has the Vine-priest. There are many among the Ol-zhaan who feel that the wisdom and judgment of the novice-master, D'ol Regle, is unsurpassed in all Green-sky."

And so the excellent and perceptive young novice, D'ol Salaat, had been dispatched back to the novice hall where he could keep watch over the two younger offenders, and D'ol Regle prepared himself for a long night of careful planning. But as he planned, his thoughts returned repeatedly to the question of D'ol Falla—and what, if anything, she would do with the information that had been given to her. Surely she would not hesitate to move against so flagrant an offense because it involved her protégé, D'ol Raamo. And if she did hesitate, if she in fact neglected to do that which was only right and necessary under the circumstances—what would be the outcome? Would not the Ol-zhaan see, at last, that it was time to choose a new Vine-priest, one who was quick in judgment and decisive action, when such action was necessary to protect the well-being of all Green-sky.

The seventh hour came and, arising from his uncomfortable resting place, D'ol Regle prepared himself for the day's demands. He had, he thought, considered every possibility and had formulated plans to deal with any eventuality, no matter how catastrophic. But even in his wildest imaginings he had not begun to foresee the terrible choices that would be forced upon him by the day's events.

The eighth hour had not yet run its course when D'ol Salaat returned, his round face pale and quivering and his eyes so glazed with emotion that they resembled the embroidered eyes of faces in a tapestry. For several minutes he seemed unable to speak, either from breathlessness due to the excessive haste with which he had come, or to the difficulty of putting into words, events so outside the realm of reason and reality. When he had, at last, gained control of his voice, he began to unfold an incredible story.

Having left D'ol Regle, the night before, D'ol Salaat had returned to the novice hall where he had stationed himself in the common room where he could observe the doorways that led to the nid-chambers of both D'ol Raamo and D'ol Genaa. There he had waited, wakeful, but perhaps dozing occasionally until shortly before the seventh hour. At that time he had observed D'ol Genaa emerge from her nid-chamber and enter that of D'ol Raamo. After only a moment she reappeared, seemingly agitated and hurriedly left the novice hall heading in the direction of the central platform of the grove. Following at a safe distance, D'ol Salaat had observed her meeting on the platform with D'ol Neric. For some minutes the two of them remained on the platform, talking in low voices and glancing around them, as if expecting the arrival of some one else, probably their accomplice, D'ol

Raamo. But no one else appeared and finally they had approached the entrance of the Vine-priest's palace, where the tendril lattice had already been removed from the entry. In spite of the earliness of the hour, the glow of lighted lamps was visible from within. They entered the palace and, hurrying after them, D'ol Salaat had entered also. Staying just far enough behind to be sure he was not seen, he followed them as they moved forward, slowly, as if unsure of their destination. Most of the huge palace was still in darkness, but a few glowing honey lamps seemed to have been hung to illuminate a pathway that led upward through halls and up rampways. At last, having reached a very narrow hallway with a secret entrance, which had been left open, his quarry began to move very slowly and quietly, and the sound of voices could be heard coming from just ahead. They stopped then, and for a long time stood still, apparently listening to what was being said in the room beyond.

Although he edged as close as he dared, D'ol Salaat was unable to hear the words of the speakers, but he was certain that one of the voices was that of D'ol Falla, while the other was probably that of D'ol Raamo. After many minutes the two who had been standing silently in the doorway entered the room and began to take part in the conversation of the first two speakers. At that point, D'ol Salaat dared to come closer and, approaching to just outside the doorway, which seemed to lead into a chamber hollowed out of an enormous grundtrunk, he was able to hear most of what was being said.

He had not been able to hear everything, and some of the words used were without meaning to him, but it was apparent that the four were making plans, to do something very strange and mysterious. They spoke, D'ol Salaat said of "releasing the Erdlings" and of the "dream of D'ol Nesh-om."

When, at last, D'ol Salaat ceased to speak, D'ol Regle sat for a long time in stunned silence. It was obvious that a plot was afoot that would, if allowed to succeed, destroy everything for which D'ol Wissen had labored; everything, in fact, that had for so long protected all of Green-sky from unthinkable risks and dangers. And it was also apparent that the greatly honored D'ol Falla was, herself, a part of this evil plot.

For many minutes D'ol Regle sat, deep in thought, while his messenger stood respectfully before him, swaying a little from time to time, as his eyes rolled upward with exhaustion. At last the novice master spoke.

"D'ol Salaat!" he said abruptly, startling the half-dozing novice, "Take the hallway to your left and continue down it until you come to the second archway. In the chamber beyond are my helpers, the Kindar who are assigned to my service; they will be engaged in their morning food-taking. Inform the two Kindar men called Tarn and Pino that they are to report to me here in the reception hall on the ninth hour. Tell them that they are to accompany me on a mission of great importance.

CHAPTER TWELVE

The blessing of down-filled comforter supported by the living strength of tendril, received her, and sighing deeply, D'ol Falla surrendered her tired body to the solace of her nid. She was exhausted, weak and trembling and giddy with exhaustion. Her nid swayed softly, and the tightly drawn night shades tempered the soft green light of midday to a tender, muted glow. But although her body gave itself up with immense gratitude to repose, her mind refused to surrender itself to sleep. Instead it raced on and on, alternately turning back in wonder to the beginning, and then racing forward into the frightening uncertainties of the future.

It had all begun only the evening before, soon after the first fall of rain, when the pudgy-faced young novice called D'ol Salaat had presented himself before her. And while he recounted his astounding story, it had become clear that the time had come—that she could wait no longer to act upon her faith in the vision of Nesh-om, or else to retreat into the living death of the recent past.

It had been, indeed, a living death. A slow gradual dying—of the Spirit first, and then of Love and Joy—of all the holy gifts proclaimed by D'ol Nesh-om in the early days of Green-sky. She had not even seen them go. Insulated by power and by the great honors that had come to her, she had for many years been unaware, or at least had tried to be. Until at last, only a few years before, she had begun to be tormented by a strange restlessness, a yearning for the gifts of the Spirit that she had once possessed.

It was then that she had begun to try to regain that which had once been hers—by fasting and meditation, by ritual and discipline, by every means she had ever encountered. It was this search that had led her to the careful study of the ancient records of the Forgotten, and it was through that study she began to develop a compelling interest in the great controversy between the two great Ol-zhaan leaders, D'ol Wissen and D'ol Nesh-om. It was they who had brought a shipload of children to Green-sky when their home planet had been on the verge of destruction. Searching carefully through the ancient records, she had confronted the dilemma that had presented itself to the two great leaders when this first generation of Kindar reached maturity. Should these children, the last survivors of a beautiful and complex civilization that had destroyed itself utterly by violence, be made aware of their past and entrusted with their future. Or should they, having learned to live for the Love and Joy of the present, continue in innocence for their own protection.

Haunted by her growing conviction that Nesh-om had been right, and that the imprisonment of his followers below the Root had been a great evil, D'ol Falla had tried cautiously to discover if there were any among her fellow Geets-kel who shared her feelings. But it soon became apparent that, while a few seemed to have some doubts concerning the justice of what had been done in the past, none seemed ready, now, to risk a change.

An then, one night, a vision or foretelling had come to her, and a voice, which she seemed to know as that of D'ol Nesh-om, spoke to her and told her of a Chosen who would, by his very existence, break the bonds of pride and fear. You will know him by his gifts of the Spirit, the voice had told her, and by the two who will accompany him and give to his promise, motion and direction.

Soon afterwards, she had heard of the child Raamo D'ok and had worked for his choosing; but when he was at last among the Ol-zhaan, she had been uncertain. Uncertain for her own faith in the vision, and also of Raamo, since his gifts seemed to be slight, and she did not yet know of his connection with the others—the forceful young Neric and the brilliant girl, Genaa.

And so she hesitated, waiting and hoping for some sign or portent, until that very night—and the sudden appearance of the officious D'ol Salaat. She had known then that she could delay no longer and, still tormented by uncertainty and fear, she had reached out desperately in mind-touch, summoning Raamo to come to her. And against all reason and logic, he had heard and come.

But she had still doubted—not D'ol Nesh-om's vision of a humanity evolved beyond the possibility of violence—but her own, which had led her to the artless, clear-eyed boy who stood before her. So she had tested him—tempting him with a tool of violence—and he had passed the test. And then the others had come, Neric and Genaa, and fullfilled the rest of the vision, and she saw at last that the time had come. The time for an end, and a new beginning.

They had begun by making plans. The morning was

advancing and there was great need for haste, but the plans had grown with painful slowness—constructed with difficulty out of widely differing attitudes and convictions. Trembling with eagerness, the intense young Neric had, at first, insisted that the proper course of action would be to go directly and immediately to the Kindar.

"We could go down to the large branchways of Orbora and gather groups of Kindar around us and tell them the truth. Tell them everything. About how their ancestors were brought to this planet to escape the violent destruction of their ancestral home, and how they have been protected from all knowledge of even the possibility of violence, and how the two great leaders, Wissen and Nesh-om, disagreed concerning their right to know the truth, and that that disagreement led to the imprisonment below the Root of all those who felt that, whatever the risk, the truth belonged to all the Kindar. And how the Pash-shan, whom they had been taught to fear, were not really monsters but only the descendents of those first few prisoners. And—"

"Wait, wait a moment, Neric," Genaa said. "Stop and think. Do you really believe that the Kindar will be able to so quickly accept such shattering revelations? After generations of avoiding any thought or feeling that might lead to conflict or confusion, do you really think they can be asked to give up their faith in the Ol-zhaan as well as their fear of the Pash-shan, simply because we ask them to?"

"But if we had proof—?"

"What proof? What can we offer them as proof?"

"We have—D'ol Falla. With D'ol Falla one of us—"

"No," D'ol Falla had interrupted. "I'm afraid my

word will not be enough. Not if the others—the other Ol-zhaan, led by the Geets-kel—choose to deny what we have said. It would be easy for D'ol Regle to convince not only the Kindar but the Ol-zhaan as well that my mind has been weakened by the weight of years. I've heard, in fact, that he has already been hinting that such might be the case, whenever he has an audience that might be sympathetic to his cause."

"His cause?" Neric asked.

"Yes," D'ol Falla had said. "The great cause that would elevate the worthy D'ol Regle to his rightful position as high priest of the Vine, and bestow on the aged D'ol Falla the blessing of a long overdue rest from such great responsibility. It is easy to guess what he would do if I were to go to the Kindar with wild accusations. He would simply announce that old age had rendered me mentally incompetent, and that you three, being very young and overly impressed by my prestige and position, had allowed yourselves to be caught up in my delusions."

"Yes," Genaa said. "And when we disappeared, as my father did, the Kindar would simply eat a few more Berries and try not to consider the fate of Ol-zhaan who are flawed by age or youth, or other human failings."

"But what would you have us do then?" Neric said impatiently. "Raamo, what would you suggest?"

"I think you are right in saying that there must be proof," Raamo said. "We must have living proof—"

"My father," Genaa cried suddenly. "If we could bring my father back from below the Root. He was well known in Orbora, and the Ol-zhaan pronounced him taken by the Pash-shan more than two years ago. Surely if he reappeared and told his story—"

"Yes," D'ol Falla said excitedly. "I think you are right, Genaa. If it is living proof that is needed, I can think of none better than a living Hiro D'anhk."

After only a moment's hesitation, Neric, too, agreed. "Good," he said. "Good. Will you go with us, D'ol Falla, to show us the way to the opening in the Root?" Even as he spoke, Neric was on his feet and turning towards the open door; but at D'ol Falla's restraining gesture, he returned to his chair and addressed himself impatiently to the matter of plans and precautions.

It would be, they had decided, necessary to keep their conspiracy a secret for as long as possible. Therefore it was decided that only Neric and Genaa would be sent to bring Hiro D'anhk back from below the Root. To preserve the appearance of normalcy, D'ol Falla would remain in her palace, and Raamo would return to the Novice Hall. There he would go about his usual schedule of classes and lessons, and D'ol Falla would explain Genaa's absence by reporting that she had been summoned to a special period of service in the Vine-priest's palace. Since Neric was no longer a novice, and his comings and goings were less strictly scheduled, his absence would less likely be noted.

"Perhaps you should take Teera with you," Raamo had said, but Neric quickly disagreed.

"No. We can go much more quickly without her. And besides, she would not know the way from the opening in the Root to the inhabited areas of Erda. It may well be a long and tiring and dangerous journey. There is no need to expose the child to such danger. If we are successful, she will soon enough be reunited with her parents."

Thus it was agreed that Neric and Genaa should go

alone on a journey that never willingly had been taken by any inhabitant of Green-sky since the days of D'ol Wissen and the spreading of the Root. Equipped only with a map that D'ol Falla hastily sketched for them on a small grundleaf, they left the palace of the high priest of the Vine just as the warm rays of the sun began to slant in across the glideways of Orbora.

Watching them go, D'ol Falla had suddenly been overwhelmed by the realization of what she had done. The die was cast, and there was no returning to the peaceful security of the past. What lay ahead was entirely unpredictable, but it was certain to be difficult and dangerous beyond imagining. Suddenly she felt very old and tired and very frightened.

"You are tired, D'ol Falla," Raamo had said. He was staring at her with his strangely luminous eyes, and she knew that she had not been blocking and that he had been pensing her weakness and uncertainty. "Let me help you to your nid-chamber," he had offered.

"No," she had said. "I will rest here a moment first, near the window. I wish to speak to you a few moments longer, before you return to the Novice Hall."

When she was seated, propped comfortably among many pillows, she had spoken to Raamo of her fears and uncertainty. "I am afraid," she said, "of failing, and of what might be done by those who will oppose us. And I am, also, fearful of our success."

"Then you are sorry for what we have done?" Raamo asked. "Do you think we decided wrongly?"

"No," she said, without hesitation. "I am certain that our decision was right. I feel unsure of many things just now, but I am most certain that the gifts of the Spirit are stunted when knowledge is restricted in any way, and for any reason. D'ol Wissen was right when he said that innocence is a charm that protects against great evils, but what he did not see is that it is a charm whose enchantment is meant to last for a season only. To prolong its use when the season is finished, is to transform its power into a force for evil—a great and deadly evil."

As she spoke, Raamo had sunk slowly to the floor before the divan on which she rested. His eyes had never left her face, and she could feel the force of his Spirit reaching out, not only for her words, but for the deeper meanings that underlay them. When she ceased speaking, he remained as he was for a long time. At last he sighed, and spoke.

"Yes," he said. "I see. I see that we had no choice but to try—to try to tell the Kindar the truth and free the Erdlings. But why do you say you fear our success?"

"Because I am old and tired; and no matter how great our success, it will not be accomplished without pain and turmoil. There is never great change and growth without pain, even when the change is good and necessary. But it is the pain that I fear—that and the Geets-kel."

"But what can they do?" Raamo asked. "When the truth has been told, how can they take it away?"

"It is possible that they will learn too soon of our plans, before we can take the truth to the Kindar. There are those among the Geets-kel who would not hesitate to do terrible things to prevent the loss of their honor and power. And even if we are able to reach the Kindar with the truth, it is possible that the Geets-kel might be able to turn the Kindar against us, and against the Erdlings, by the use of methods such as were often used in the days before the Flight, on the ancestral planet.

It was common then for leaders to emphasize differences and distances in order to make evil use of the natural instinct to fear the unknown."

"Do you really think the Kindar could—could lift their hands against the Erdlings?"

D'ol Falla sighed, shaking her head. "I don't know. It would not have been possible for the Kindar of the early days who were Spirit-blessed by the teachings of D'ol Nesh-om. But the Kindar of today have been corrupted by ignorance, and it is in ignorance that fear grows into hatred."

There had followed a long silence as D'ol Falla sank into troubled reverie. At last, speaking almost to herself, she had said, "What can be done in the face of evil power?" Then, turning to the boy she had said, "Raamo, when I tested you last night in the Forgotten, by threatening your life with the tool of violence, I felt that in you D'ol Nesh-om's dream was vindicated—that a time might come, indeed, when all humankind might be free forever from the instinct for violence. But I see now that we may be forced to face the ancient dilemma. What does one do, Raamo, when evil threatens not only your own life but the lives of others?"

"I don't know," Raamo said.

"There must be an answer," D'ol Falla had said. "Long ago, in the days before the Flight, there were those who believed that all violence was evil, and who died quietly for their belief, but there was no answer in their dying. The answer must lie elsewhere. You must seek for the answer, Raamo."

The boy had nodded earnestly. "I don't know where to seek for it," he had said. "But I think—it will be. The answer will be." And then suddenly he had smiled delightedly, and in answer to D'ol Falla's questioning look he had explained, "Like the song," he said. "The nonsense song that children sing. It used to be my favorite," and he had begun to sing, "Then will the answer be—then it will be."

His voice was clear and pure and not yet deepened by manhood, and listening, D'ol Falla felt herself burdened by deep, unreasoned shadows, shadows darkened by foreboding, and also by pity. He is a child, she thought, only a child.

He had gone soon afterwards, and it was not until then that D'ol Falla had, at last, risen from the divan and made her way to her own chamber and the comfort of her nid. Midday had already been approaching, and in spite of her exhaustion she had not been able to fall asleep, or to keep her mind from racing restlessly through hopes and fears. But when sleep finally came, like a blessing, it did not last for long.

D'ol Falla had slept for, perhaps, almost an hour when she was aroused by one of the Kindar serving women.

"D'ol Falla," the voice was saying as, with great difficulty, she struggled back to consciousness from the depths of exhausted slumber. "Forgive me, Honored One, but the novice master D'ol Regle awaits you in the small reception hall. I told him that you were sleeping, but he would not wait. He insists that he must see you now, on a matter of great urgency."

And so D'ol Falla rose from her nid and made her way to the reception hall where D'ol Regle waited to tell her that Pomma D'ok, the sister of D'ol Raamo, and the young Pash-shan known as Teera, had been taken prisoner by the Geets-kel.

"We have met," D'ol Regle said. "The Geets-kel have met in council, and we have agreed that the lives of the two children will be forfeit if any attempt is made to free the Pash-shan or to corrupt the Kindar by burdening them with evil knowledge."

And so it had come, the moment that she had so feared and for which she was so unprepared, the moment of evil choices when life or death hangs in the balance.

CHAPTER THIRTEEN

The early morning movement of Kindar from nid-place to place of service was at its highest when Neric and Genaa set forth from the palace of the high priest of the Vine. Before them the central platform of the Temple Grove was full of hurrying people, for the most part Kindar workers on their way to the temples or Ol-zhaan palaces. Pausing for a moment under the arched doorway of D'ol Falla's palace, it occurred to Neric to wonder what they would think if they knew—if the passing Kindar knew that, here, before their very eyes a journey was beginning that had never been made before—a voluntary journey to the dark regions below the Root.

"What would they say if we told them?" he said softly to Genaa. "If we told them we were on our way to the tunnels of the Pash-shan, and that we would return with a Kindar who has been living among the Pash-shan?"

Genaa's smile was quick and hard. "What would they say if we told them we were on our way to visit the land of the dead? They would find it no less unthinkable. In either case we would be judged mad, or Berry-sotted. Come, let us hurry. It is probably safer now when we can mingle with the Kindar."

As they started across the bustling platform, they were careful to steer away from the occasional gleam of a white shuba. Thus they reached the outer gateway of the Temple Grove without a face-to-face encounter with any Ol-zhaan. They were then on the wide rampway that led down to the mid-heights of Stargrund. From there a long glide would take them through the center of Orbora to a landing on one of the great lower branchways of Skygrund, the most westerly of the giant grund trees that supported the city.

At that hour the glidepaths were well traveled and, as Genaa and Neric drifted downwards, they passed through groups of Kindar of all ages, dressed in shubas of every shade and hue. Groups of children, dressed in brilliant colors floated by, their light bodies so buoyant that they seemed scarcely to be descending, as they filled the air around them with the sound of their singing, laughing voices. Since it was unusual for Ol-zhaan to be outside the Temple Grove at such an early hour, many of the older Kindar glanced curiously at the two young Ol-zhaan. A few lifted upturned palms as they passed by, in the Kindar gesture of respect and honor.

"Let us hope that they are not Temple servers," Neric said. "Or, at least, that they are not in the service of one of the Geets-kel."

Genaa drifted closer, nodding. "Yes," she said. "It occurs to me that I should have removed my tabard. As a novice, I am more easily identifiable, since we are so few."

By then, however, they were already in the mid-heights of Sky-grund, and it was necessary to drop swiftly, circling the enormous trunk and coming to a quick landing on the great lower branchway that stretched out in a southerly direction. From there they would walk, following at first the established forest branchway, until they reached the third outlying grund tree.

Situated as it was on the farthest outskirts of the city, the branchway, although wide and level, was sparsely inhabited. As Genaa and Neric walked quickly down its great length, they saw only two small nid-places, and passed no fellow pedestrians, either Kindar or Ol-zhaan. Soon they were among thickly grown end branches, which intermingled with the end branches of the first outer-forest grund.

They were now on an established branchway, which led out through the open forest towards the neighboring city of Ninegrund. Such branchways, developed mainly for the use of porters too heavily laden to glide, were kept cleared and marked and equipped where necessary with ladders and rampways. As Neric and Genaa approached the trunk of the first grund, they entered a rampway leading around the trunk to the beginning of its most southerly branch. When they had, in this manner, reached the third outlying grund, Neric stopped and unrolled the grundleaf map. It was here, from this grund, according to D'ol Falla, that all Vine Processions that carried drugged bodies of exiled Kindar made their descent to the forest floor.

"D'ol Falla spoke of anchors, loops to which the rope ladder were attached," Genaa said.

"But we have no ladders," Neric protested.

"Don't we?" Genaa said. "I thought perhaps you had thought to bring one in your belt pouch." Her pointed smile softened just in time to prevent Neric's tentative frown from hardening into anger. "I only meant that finding the loops would prove that we were indeed at the

right place. Since the map centers around the place of descent, it will be very important to find the exact spot."

Nodding sharply Neric rolled the map and led the way around the rampway. And soon afterwards, at the base of a westerly branch, they came upon loops of braided tendril attached to the stumps of side branches.

"Ah," Neric said, pointing. "There they are." Approaching the edge of the branchway, he gazed down the great towering trunk, down and down to where the dense vegetation of the forest floor was transformed by distance to a shadowy carpet of darkest green. "It's strange—very strange," he said.

"Yes. Strange—and horrible." Genaa was standing beside him.

"Horrible?" Neric asked. "I meant that it seems strange to look below without fear—or guilt. To know that there is no Pash-shan lying in wait below the Root—that all the warnings were needless—makes it seem so entirely different. It even looks different—almost beautiful. It no longer seems horrible, to me, at least."

"I did not mean the forest floor," Genaa said. "I meant this place. This place where all the Verban, drugged and helpless, were lowered down into—into death." Genaa's voice was taut and brittle. "Death," she said again, "at least to everything they had known and loved."

"Come, Genaa. It does no good to think about it." Neric pulled her away from the branch edge, but she resisted, her body tense and rigid, her gaze as fixed as that of a foreseer in deep trance. "Come," he urged, "think instead of what we are doing, and how, if we are successful, all the Verban will be restored to Green-sky and to all those who loved them."

"Yes," Genaa said at last, shuddering as she turned her eyes away.

"We must look now for a heavy stand of Vine—" Neric was saying when suddenly he stopped. "No! There is no longer any need to climb down cautiously. We can glide. We can glide down to the forest floor without fear of landing within reach of death-dealing claws."

And so, without fear, Neric and Genaa launched themselves from the lowest branch level and drifted downward, as no Kindar had ever done before. After spiraling slowly through the soft damp air, they landed at the base of the same grund, directly below the place where the Vine-priests had attached their ladders. Once there, they unfurled their map again and studied it carefully.

From the circle that represented the trunk of the grund, D'ol Falla had drawn a line that extended due west, past a double trunk, where two grunds had come up so close together that their trunks had merged. Beyond the double circle, the line turned sharply to the north. Turning to the west, the two moved forward through great fern, which, arching high above their heads, made it impossible to see for any distance. But they had not gone far when they glimpsed the towering double column of the merged grunds. Circling the enormous trunk, they turned north. After a short time they reached the next landmark shown on the grundleaf map —a great boulder, gray and forbidding. At its base they turned again to the west.

Now they found themselves on a narrow path that wound its way through dense fern and heavy growths of ground vine. The light was dim, and the air was heavy with strange rich odors, so overwhelming that they seemed to touch and caress the skin. The earth below their feet was soft and spongy with no sign of the radiating ridges that indicated that the grillwork of Root lay near the surface of the soil. The path forked twice and, following the map's markings, they each time took the right hand fork, and in a few minutes they found themselves approaching another boulder.

"There it is," Neric whispered. "And see, there is another and another. We have found the place."

It was here that D'ol Falla's map ended, at a place where three boulders set close together, forming a triangle. At the center of that triangle lay the opening in the Root. As the two young Ol-zhaan stepped through the narrow opening between the boulders, they saw before them a pit, several feet across and a little deeper than the height of a tall man. The bottom of the pit seemed to be full of fallen leaves. Without hesitating, Neric stepped forward and jumped lightly down to the bottom; a moment later Genaa landed beside him.

Neric was already on his knees, raking up the thick layer of dead vegetation. Beneath the leaves, the earth was loose and soft, and suddenly Neric gasped, clutching the fingers of his right hand.

"What is it?" Genaa asked.

"The Root," Neric said. "I am never prepared for its coldness. See, it lies just here."

"And here another branch crosses. D'ol Falla said it forms a square of dimensions large enough to allow the passage of even the largest man, and the opening is covered by a shield of metal. The shield must lie here, between the branches."

The metal shield, which had once been a part of the flying chamber in which the Flight was made, was soon laid bare. Grasping it from each side, they were able to lift it away. As they placed it against the wall of the pit, they saw that its underside was roughly textured and fashioned to resemble the earthy roof of the tunnel so that, seen from below, it would give no hint of what lay above.

With the cover removed, Neric and Genaa stared down into a gaping hole of incredible darkness—a blackness that seemed utterly different from the soft breathing shadows of the forest night. Looking down into that well of oblivion, it seemed almost as if it would not be possible to move, or even to breathe in such darkness. Leaning down, Genaa thrust her arm as far as she could into the hole. She held it there for a moment and then removed it, staring at it strangely. Glancing up she saw that Neric, too, was staring at her hand.

Genaa's smile attempted self-mockery, but it was not entirely successful. "I almost expected—" she began.

"I know," Neric said, "that it would be gone. That it would have been dissolved by the darkness. I felt that, too."

They continued to stare silently into the black hole for a long time before Neric spoke again. "I wish we had thought to bring a honey lantern. Do you think we should go back for one?"

"I was thinking of that also, but we would have to wait then until dusk when the moon moths begin to fly. I think we must go on—through the darkness. We will feel our way—as the Verban do when they waken below the Root. But we must think of a way to mark our path, so that we will be able to return to this spot after we have reached the Erdlings and found my father."

Neric recalled at once what he and Raamo had done when they first came to the forest floor. They had marked their path with fern fronds. No better solution presented itself, so it was agreed upon. Climbing out of the pit, Neric and Genaa hastily set about gathering large armloads of fronds, which they bound into two large bundles with strands of ground vine. With the bundles slung over their shoulders, they climbed back down into the pit and stood, once more, at the opening in the Root.

"Are we ready?" Genaa said. "Will you go first, or shall I?"

"I will," Neric said. "But it has just occurred to me that perhaps we should look first for some roots and mushrooms. We may be many days in the tunnels before we are found and—"

"I have a little pan-fruit in my belt pouch," Genaa said, "and Teera said that water is plentiful in the tunnels—that there are many small springs and streams. I think we should not delay any longer."

"Yes, you are right," Neric agreed. He knelt down at the very edge of the opening, and leaning forward he peered down into the darkness. "I think I can see the tunnel floor," he announced after a moment. "It's not far." Swinging his legs over the edge, he pushed forward —and disappeared into the darkness.

Watching, Genaa was suddenly gripped by cold fingers of fear. It seemed as if Neric had been swallowed —gulped down into the earth. But then, as she leaned forward, a dim, shadowy face appeared slowly, floating up out of the darkness.

"I lit on my knees," Neric said. He lifted up his hands, and they came almost to the mouth of the hole. "See, it's not far to the tunnel floor. Take my hands as you jump."

A moment later they were standing side-by-side on the tunnel floor. Above their heads there was light—a small square of warm inviting radiance. But all around them was darkness and a cold, unearthly silence. As the moments passed, the dark silence seemed to seep into their hearts, and minds, smothering every thought and feeling in a dense fog of foreboding.

CHAPTER FOURTEEN

Teera finished the last morsel of nut porridge with fruit sauce and licked the spoon. "They surely can't mean to hurt us," she said, "or they wouldn't bother to feed us so well. Don't you think so, Pomma?"

Pomma, who was still eating, looked up at Teera curiously. "Hurt us?" she said. "You keep talking about their hurting us. Why would they do that—and how? How would they—" Pomma's voice wavered and her eyes fell. The images that came to her mind when she thought of hurting were vague and indistinct, but definitely uncomfortable to think about.

"Hurting" Teera said. "You know." She made a gesture of striking and then of kicking. "Hasn't anyone ever hurt you—like other children, when you were playing and someone—" She swung her hand towards Pomma's face, stopping just in time to prevent contact.

"Oh that," Pomma said. "Like in a dance when someone's hand swings around and hits your face? But we don't call that hurting. We call it accident. Always when anyone pains you at the Garden, it is called an accident. That means that you are paining but no one meant to, and that everyone is sorry." Pomma smiled, remembering how it was when there was an accident at the Garden—how everyone gathered around both the one who was paining and the one who had caused the pain and caressed and soothed them both, making a Ceremony of Comfort. It was often almost a Joy to be an accident at the Garden.

Teera sighed. "But don't they ever do it on purpose because they are angry or because you have something they want?"

Pomma looked down, her cheeks reddening. "You shouldn't say things like that," she said.

Teera sighed again more loudly. "All right," she said. "But the Ol-zhaan do hurt people. At least they hurt Erdlings and the Verban. And it was the Ol-zhaan who took us away from your nid-place and shut us up here. And it must be because we know that there really aren't any Pash-shan, and they are afraid that we will tell."

"But we could promise them that we wouldn't tell."

"I don't think they would believe us. Because we might tell without meaning to, or we might forget about promising. I don't think they would believe a promise, at least not enough to let us go."

"What do you think they will do with us then?"

"I think they might put us down below the Root, like they do the Verban." Teera spoke rather cheerfully, thinking of the surprised delight of her parents and clan-siblings, and of how fascinated they would be with Pomma, a Kindar child. But at that moment her musing ended abruptly, interrupted by a sudden awareness of fear and despair. Pomma's face was blank, her eyes wide and expressionless; but Teera could pense her terror. It was not until then that Teera realized what it would mean to Pomma to be sent below the Root.

Throwing her arms around Pomma, she caressed her soothingly, crooning words of comfort; but Pomma's fear died slowly.

"I was wrong," Teera told her. "I didn't remember that you are a Kindar, and the sister of an Ol-zhaan. They would never put you below the Root. Please, Pomma, don't think of it anymore. Let's think of other things—like, how well I am learning to Five-Pense. Shall we Five-Pense, or do you want to play Garden, like we did yesterday?"

Pomma raised her eyes and, Teera, pensing a flicker of interest amid the despairing gloom pushed her advantage. "Yes," she said enthusiastically. "Let's do the kiniporting practice, the kind we did yesterday. Remember what happened yesterday, Pomma? Let's see if we can do it again."

I'm not sure we can do it again," Pomma said, but her fear was behind her now, her eyes shining. "I don't know how it happened. It wasn't at all like it is at the Garden."

"Wasn't it? Not at all like the Garden?" Teera was obviously disappointed.

"Not really. It's only the cylinder that is supposed to move towards you."

Teera sighed.

"But then," Pomma added comfortingly, "we don't really have the right kind of cylinders or table. At the Garden the tables are frond-woven and suspended. And this table—" She stopped, and leaning back in her chair to get a better view she examined the table at which they were seated. It was fashioned of inlaid pan-wood and mounted on a massive pedestal, ornately carved to resemble a heavily interwoven growth of Vine-stem.

"But we could do it like they do at the Garden if we

had the right kind of cylinders and table. Don't you think?" Teera asked.

Pomma nodded. "Yes," she said. "I'm sure we could."

There was a silence and then, leaning forward, Teera stared at Pomma intently. "What was it? What was it that happened yesterday?"

"I don't know," Pomma answered slowly. "But I don't think it was kiniporting. Babies kiniport leaves and feathers, and, at the Garden you kiniport cylinders. But not tables—not pan-wood tables."

They continued to stare into each other's eyes, their faces glowing, and for just a moment it seemed about to happen again: the force flowing, swelling, and then it faded.

When Teera spoke again, her voice had become a whisper. "Was it—is it—could it be—uniforce?"

The light in Pomma's eyes stilled and deepened, but she shook her head firmly. "No," she said. "No one can uniforce anymore."

They nodded, still staring into each other's eyes, pensing in unison, Let's see if we can do it again.

At that same hour, while the two small captives were beginning to play their intriguing game, D'ol Regle was sitting down to his morning food-taking in a chamber almost directly below the one in which they were imprisoned. The secret chamber was formed by the highest dome in the palace of the novice master and could be entered only through D'ol Regle's private suite of rooms. Except for the novice-master and his two serving men, Tarn and Pino, no one in all Green-sky knew of the secret room or of the exact whereabouts of the two children. There were others, of course, who knew of their disappearance; but what they knew varied according to what they needed to know, no more and no less. In the long hours of the night in which D'ol Regle had learned of the conspiracy, he had planned it all with extreme care and thoroughness. From the very beginning every step had been made with precision and for good reason.

The two Kindar serving men had been chosen, for instance, from the many who served in the palace, for certain qualities that made them uniquely suited for the great responsibility. They were simple men, proud of their service in high places, and intensely loyal to the person and power of D'ol Regle. They were, D'ol Regle mused, true Kindar, personifications of the time-honored Kindar virtues of innocence and faith. Not once since the morning when he had asked them to fetch two large portage baskets, and to accompany him on an exceedingly strange mission, had they questioned in word or manner the tasks that they had been given to do. D'ol Regle had, of course, praised them highly, indicating that the transportation of the two children to his palace was a matter of great importance and, at least for the present, of great secrecy—and that they, Tarn D'ald and Pino D'erl, would, at the proper time, be rewarded with the highest honor and acclaim. There was, D'ol Regle felt sure, no need for any apprehension concerning Tarn and Pino, no matter what transpired or what might be asked of them. And the even more intensely loyal, D'ol Salaat, had also been sworn to silence and could be relied upon.

There were others, however, whose behavior was much harder to predict. Among such there were the parents of the child Pomma, Hearba and Valdo D'ok. They had been told that the two children had been taken to the temple for special testing by the Ol-zhaan, and that such an occurrence was a thing that reflected great honor on the children and on their entire family. However, since the first day, they had not seemed to be entirely satisfied. In the short time since the children had been taken, the mother had twice hired a messenger to carry to D'ol Regle an inquiry concerning the children's welfare, and the length of time that they would be kept in the Temple Grove. But whatever their suspicions, the parents of Pomma were only Kindar and no real threat to D'ol Regle's plans. Of more concern, was the strange behavior of some among the Geets-kel, themselves.

D'ol Regle had called a meeting of the Geets-kel immediately after the two children had been safely installed in the hidden chamber. They had assembled quickly, sixteen of them in all. They were, without exception, men and women of high honor, well versed in all the skills of leadership, and fully aware of the great responsibilities of their high offices. And yet, when they had been told, when D'ol Regle had made clear to them the catastrophic nature of the danger facing them—and all Green-sky—there were some among them who seemed unable to see clearly and act decisively. There was, for instance, D'ol Wassou, who repeatedly demanded that D'ol Falla be summoned to the meeting to state her case before her fellow Geets-kel and to take part in their decision.

That old Wassou should be so unreasonable was perhaps to be expected, considering the fact that he was a fellow Vine-priest with D'ol Falla. But the reaction of D'ol Birta had been harder to understand. D'ol Birta, high priest of the Garden, and the final authority in all matters pertaining to the education and Spirit-growth of the Kindar, was a woman of vigorous and forceful character. None among the Ol-zhaan seemed more perfectly suited to the high honor and responsibility of her position. And yet, when D'ol Regle had finished explaining the steps that would have to be taken if the rebels refused to listen to reason, D'ol Birta's behavior was surprisingly unsuitable. Rising suddenly from her place at the council table, she had begun to speak in a voice that wavered strangely.

"I will take no part in such horrors," she had said. "I will not oppose you, D'ol Regle, if the others feel that there is no alternative. But I could never agree to it, never take part in it." And turning hastily, she had stumbled blindly from the chamber.

The council had been a long and painful one, but when it had at last been concluded, D'ol Regle's plan had been accepted. And, since there was no time to lose, he had immediately put it into effect.

Hurrying to the palace of the high priest of the Vine, D'ol Regle had entered unannounced and had made his way directly to the secret chamber known as the Forgotten. Fortunately, years before he had been entrusted with a key, the only duplicate of the one that D'ol Falla carried always on her person. The palace was huge and rambling, and D'ol Falla kept few serving people, so it was with little difficulty that D'ol Regle had reached the hidden chamber without being observed, completed his business there, and returned to the entry way. There he blew upon the entry flute, until at last an elderly serving woman had appeared. And not long afterwards, in answer to his summons, D'ol Falla, herself, had entered the reception hall.

Reliving that moment—the moment of confrontation

—aroused such strong emotions that for many minutes Dol Regle's beautifully prepared breakfast lay untouched upon his table board. Strange unnamed feelings of great intensity filled his mind and heart as he thought over what he had said and how Dol Falla had reacted.

At last, sighing, he pushed himself back from the table and, after carefully wiping his hands on a silken napkin, he crossed the large richly furnished chamber. From the western end of his balcony he could, by leaning slightly forward, catch a glimpse of the graceful flights and rampways of the Vine Palace. It was, indeed, a thing of beauty, and it would undoubtedly soon be his —but for the time being it was still the abode of D'ol Falla. Staring intently, he found himself wishing that he could image—like an infant Kindar. Wishing that he could see D'ol Falla now, now that she knew. Now that she had had time to reach a full realization of the dilemma that confronted her. When he had faced her, she had reacted with a prideful reserve which she had managed to maintain until he had left her presence. But what would she be doing now? How would she appear— now that she had had ample time to consider the full extent of the disaster which she had brought down upon herself—now that she knew that all her treacherous plans were discovered and that her power and honor, even her life, lay like a fragile mistborne blossom in the hands of D'ol Regle?

And at the same time, while the two young hostages played their games and practiced the Spirit-skills of their ancestors, and while the novice master brooded on his balcony, D'ol Falla was waiting in the small reception room of her palace, trying to prepare herself for the pain that lay just ahead. Raamo would soon be arriving, and it would be necessary to tell him of D'ol Regle's visit and of the message that he had come to bring. It would be necessary for her to tell Raamo that their plans were known and that his sister and the Erdling child had been abducted. And that D'ol Regle and the Geets-kel were demanding that all who had been involved in the plan to free the Erdlings submit themselves to the Geets-kel in exchange for the lives of the captive children.

Closing her eyes, D'ol Falla tried to shut her mind, if only for a moment, to the pain and turmoil that seemed to be pressing in on her from every side. She was suddenly overcome with a feeling of helplessness and of total exhaustion. It is too much, she thought, and I am too old and tired.

She had been waiting for what seemed to be a very long time, enclosed in pain and darkness, when suddenly she became aware of a faint whisper of mind-touch. Her eyes flew open to see Raamo standing before her—and as his eyes met hers the whisper become a wordless message of concern.

"What is it?" he said at last in voice-speech. "What has happened? What is it that concerns Pomma and Teera?"

Speaking slowly and with great difficulty, D'ol Falla told him of the kidnapped children, and of how D'ol Regle had come to her and told her of the Geets-kel's meeting and what had there been agreed upon. She spoke also of how D'ol Regle had entered the Vine Palace secretly and had gone into the Forgotten and taken possession of the one tool of violence that was still equipped to perform its terrible function. As she spoke, fear and horror caused by her words lay open and unblocked in Raamo's eyes and mind, causing her own voice to stumble and falter.

"Surely he could not have meant—" Raamo began. "He did not say that—"

"He said that the safety of the children depended upon our surrendering ourselves—without having spoken to anyone else of what we know. He said that you and I, Neric and Genaa must come silently and secretly to the small council chamber in the heights of the grove before rainfall this evening and there await the will of the Geets-kel."

"But Neric and Genaa are gone. They are by now below the Root. We don't know when they will return."

"Yes, I told him that. And he said that we should then wait here for their return. When they come, we are to bring them with us to the council chamber. And if they bring the Verban, Hiro D'anhk, with them, he also must accompany us to the chamber."

There was a long silence, a dark and hopeless silence, before Raamo said, "What will we do?"

"I don't know. It would be but a small sacrifice for me to surrender what little is left of my life for the safety of the children. But I cannot believe that our purpose is ours alone to surrender. And I do not know what Neric and Genaa will do when they return. But we must decide what we, you and I, will do in the meantime, and inform D'ol Regle before this evening's rainfall.

Raamo sank slowly to the floor, borne down by the weight of his despair.

"Raamo," D'ol Falla said. "It has come—the ancient dilemma. The question of what can be done in the face of evil power. In the past—before the Flight—there were those who opposed violence in violent ways, and the evil grew and spread; and there were others who sacrificed themselves in the name of peace, and the evil swallowed them and flourished. At last there was only flight. But the evil has followed us, and we can fly no farther. When I spoke of this last night, you said that you thought there was an answer. You are a child of the Spirit and must seek now for the wisdom of the Spirit. What is the answer, Raamo?"

Raamo sat where he had collapsed on the floor, his body slight and graceful as a young child's, his face blank and calm. The fear had gone from his eyes.

"The answer—will be," he said.

But hearing him, D'ol Falla could not convince herself that the words were more than the hopefulness of childhood.

CHAPTER FIFTEEN

In the blackness of the tunnels there was no way to judge the passage of time. It had been hours, many long hours, perhaps even days, since Neric and Genaa had moved slowly away from the opening in the Root and into total darkness. Inching their way forward, shuffling their feet through the rough, abrasive dirt of the tunnel floor, or sliding their hands along the dank walls, they felt their way down seemingly endless corridors of darkness. As they crept forward, they counted, and at regular intervals they left behind them a strand of fern to mark their path. Several times the sound of water trickling had led them to springs that oozed out of the tunnel walls. The water from the springs fell into rocky basins and formed small streams, which flowed along the tunnel for a short distance and then disappeared into the porous earth. Now and then they stopped to drink or to rest briefly, sitting close together for comfort against the tunnel wall. But finding themselves too restless and uneasy to relax, they were soon up and moving forward.

Again and again as she felt her way through the darkness, Genaa found herself racked and tortured by terrible imaginings. As the dark hours passed, her fear and dread grew stronger and stronger until it became a silent scream. At last it became unbearable and stopping suddenly, she reached out for Neric and pulled him to a stop.

"What is it?" he asked. "Did you hear something?"

"No." Genaa gasped. "At least not with my ears. But it's almost as if I am hearing. It's almost as if I am pensing the fear of the others. The others who groped their way down these same tunnels."

"I know." Neric said. "I too have felt it."

Strangely comforted, Genaa suddenly began to shiver. It was as if she had been, until that moment, too immobilized with fear, too lost in dread, for even that small release of tension. Grasping Neric's hands, she could feel that they, too, were trembling.

"There is no reason for such fear, I know," Genaa said. "Not for us. We could be afraid of going in circles, of not reaching the inhabited areas where we might be found by the Erdlings, but that is all. The terror that has been tormenting me is not for that. It is their fear—the Verban's. It is as if they left it behind them in these tunnels, in the rocks and earth and the cold thick air—as if it is still here, so strong and real that we cannot help feeling it."

"Yes," Neric said. "Perhaps it is so. It is like that, like the fear of the Pash-shan—the terrible unknown."

Genaa moaned softly.

"But think," Neric said. "Only think what will be done if our mission is successful. There will be no more terrible unknown, no more Pash-shan to haunt the dreams of the Kindar."

"And no more Verban, lost, blind and alone, in the lair of monsters."

When they again moved forward, Genaa found that her fear had become, not less, but more bearable. Shuffling, groping and stumbling, they went on and on for many hours until, at last, weak and exhausted, they stopped again to rest. Leaning against a thick, gnarled protrusion of grundroot, they ate a few mouthfuls of Genaa's pan-fruit and then tried to sleep. But they soon found that in spite of their exhaustion, sleep did not come quickly. It seemed to Genaa that to sleep on the cold, hard earth would be almost impossible for anyone whose body was accustomed to the soft swaying comfort of a nid. A nid—even the thought was somehow soothing. She let her mind drift with the thought, rocking, swaying into forgetfulness, and then suddenly she found herself shaken out of a deep sleep by a short strangled cry.

For a moment it seemed to Genaa that it was she, herself, who had screamed—as if the fear that had tortured her since she entered the tunnels had burst forth from her throat at last. But as full consciousness returned, she became aware that her eyes, which had for so long been blind and useless in the darkness, were no longer so. Wide open and staring, her eyes were registering light and motion. Somewhere in the darkness before her, two small lights bobbed and weaved unevenly, and in their small radius there was rapid movement, flickering and indistinct. The lights grew smaller, the movement more uncertain, and then quite suddenly they disappeared, and once again there was nothing but total darkness.

"Did you see them?" Neric's voice whispered urgently.

"Them?" Genaa said. "I saw something. I was asleep, then something woke me, a cry, I think, and I saw something—two lights in the distance. What was it?"

"I'm not certain. I saw little more than you did. But I

think it might have been people. People carrying lanterns and running. Running away from us."

"Away from us?" Genaa said, and then she understood. "It is our seals and shubas," she said. "They fear us as Ol-zhaan. Why didn't we think of it? We should have found Kindar shubas to wear before we entered the tunnels."

"Yes," Neric said, "it occurred to me, but not until we were many hours in the tunnels."

Genaa bit her lip in frustration. How could she have been so stupid. It was as if her ability to plan and reason had deserted her, now that it really mattered.

"If we had only thought to wear Kindar shubas, we would at this moment be on our way to Erda," she said. "Those Erdlings who are probably still running in terror would be guiding us, and welcoming us as newly banished Verban."

"I know," Neric said. "I know."

"What shall we do?"

"We could remove our shubas," Neric said reluctantly. The thought was troublesome and uncomfortable. Uncomfortable because of the deep pervading chill of the tunnels, and troublesome for less rational reasons. Careful training made all Kindar children fearful of venturing beyond the walls of their nid-places without the garment that protected them from the one great danger—the fall to the forest floor.

Genaa shuddered and then shook her head, realizing the instinctive and unreasoned nature of her reaction. "It's a strange place to fear falling," she said.

"Yes, but not a strange place to fear the cold," Neric said. "I am already as cold and stiff as a dead sima. Without my shuba I—"

But Genaa interrupted. "There is no need," she said. "It would be useless. The Erdlings who have seen us will soon alert all Erda to our presence, and the fact that we are Ol-zhaan. It is unlikely that they will cease to fear us because we have removed our seals and shubas. Since we have already been seen, we might just as well continue as we are. We can only hope that we will be awake when we next meet Erdlings so we can try to convince them that we mean no harm. I almost wish, now, that we had not told the Erdling, Tocar, to be silent concerning his meeting with us. He could have spread the word that there are some Ol-zhaan who are not enemies of Erda."

"True," Neric said. "But since we did not, we can only hope that we can induce the next Erdlings we meet to listen to us instead of running. It has occurred to me, however, that the next Erdlings we meet may be looking for us and have no intentions of running away."

"What do you think their intentions would be then? To accept us as Verban—or something other?"

"I don't know." Neric said. "I don't know. Except that to an Erdling, an Ol-zhaan is not a human. To them we are the curse that has imprisoned them. We are darkness and hunger and the cold barrier of the Root. They fear us because they believe we have great powers, but they have metal and fire, and the truth about the past. I do not think that they will run for long."

"Yes," Genaa said. "But if we can get them to listen, to talk to us—"

"We can try," Neric said.

Once more they began to move forward. But now they stopped more and more often to listen, straining their ears to catch even the faintest and most distant sound. But except for the occasional trickle of a spring, the silence all around them was as deep and complete as the darkness. And still the dark corridors stretched on endlessly. But they seemed larger and wider, and now and then smaller passageways branched off, leading steeply upwards. At the beginning of one of these small tunnels Neric noticed a slight difference in the quality of the air. The darkness was still complete, but he seemed to feel a faint breath of warmth and motion against his upturned face. Pulling Genaa after him, he scrambled up the steeply inclined passageway and, in only a few minutes, the blackness around them began to fade to gray; and a moment later, there appeared above them a bright rectangle of light. When the tunnel ended, they were standing below the opening of a ventilation tunnel, and directly above their heads was the grillwork of Root.

Here the Root grew in a tangled network, closely spaced. The openings were long and narrow, much too narrow to permit the passage of a human head. But standing with his face near the Root, Neric could see the light and feel the warmth and smell the living, breathing odors of the forest. Careless of the stinging cold of the Root, he thrust his arms out into the sweet forest air.

Beside him, Genaa, too, longed to breathe the free air, and comfort her skin with light and warmth. It was a fierce angry longing, full of bitterness and loss. Just as she had been overwhelmed by a fear that seemed to come from the terrors of others, she now felt herself to be suffocating—engulfed in a desperate longing, too old and deep to be only her own. Pushing Neric aside, she thrust her arms up into the free air, straining upward, her fingers spread wide as if to grasp and hold the light and warmth of the open forest.

"Come," Neric said at last. "We must go on." He

turned to go, and Genaa followed. As they made their way down the steep incline, they moved slowly, stopping often to look back towards the fading light.

Not long afterwards, moving again through a large, slightly sloping tunnel, Neric struck his foot against something hard and cold and, kneeling, he discovered a length of metal rail. Excitedly, they crept forward following the rail with their hands until it came to an end, seemingly buried in the loose debris of the tunnel floor. But a short way further on, they again encountered a length of rail not yet fully covered by earth and rockfall.

"Teera spoke of the rail systems that carry the products of the mines to the factories near the city," Neric said. "We must be getting very near to Erda."

"Perhaps. But these rails have plainly been unused for many years," Genaa said. "Who knows how far they extend. Teera said the deserted mine tunnels extend for many, many miles in all directions."

"True. But if we follow these rails we will, at least, be moving in the direction of the city."

They went on for some time, following the rail line. Ventilation tunnels became more frequent, some of them mere shafts that led almost straight up from the tunnel roof, allowing faint rays of light to penetrate to the railbed. Others, wider and more gently pitched, led up to small chambers, directly below the grillwork of Root. Most of these Genaa insisted on exploring.

"Why?" Neric asked. "We have no time to spare, nor energy. We must move on toward Erda."

"But Teera said that such places were often used by the Erdlings to set traps for lapan and other forest creatures, and as lookout posts, to watch for fallen Kindar infants. We might find an Erdling lookout posted at the end of one of these ventilation tunnels." She spoke firmly and with assurance, although she knew that it was her own consuming need to see the light and breathe the sweet warm forest air, more than any real hope of finding an Erdling sentry, that drew her tired body up the narrow passageways.

Gradually, as the long hours passed, their progress became slower and slower. The lack of food and rest began to take its toll. Not only their energy, but also their supplies of fern fronds were near an end. For some time now, they had been leaving smaller and smaller pieces of fern to mark the pathway, but even so Genaa's bundle was entirely gone, and Neric's contained only a few more long strands.

Neric's muscles had begun to quiver constantly, and his whole body ached and pained. Beside him, he could feel Genaa stumbling and slipping with almost every step. He had almost decided to suggest that they stop again to try to sleep when suddenly he realized that the darkness around him had given way to dim gray light. Rousing himself from a stupor of exhaustion, he looked around. The light was faint and uncertain but strong enough to reveal that the close surrounding walls of the tunnel seemed to have dissolved in space, and above and before him lay great, dimly lit distances. As they moved forward into what seemed to be an immense cavern, it became apparent that lanterns had been attached to the cavern wall, from which light flared and leaped in a manner quite unlike the cool steady glow of a honey lamp.

After the close confinement of the tunnels, the cavern seemed enormous. In the dim light it seemed to be peopled by strange and fearful shapes. A long breathless moment passed before it became apparent that the formations that hung down from the cavern ceiling, or reared upward from its floor, were not living things, but only masses of some hard whitish substance. Here and there, where rays of light struck their surfaces, they glittered with small points of reflected light. Farther away near the other end of the cavern, there seem to be three small pools of darkly shining water.

Their exhaustion forgotten for the moment, Neric and Genaa moved slowly forward towards the center of the cavern, entranced by the weird beauty that surrounded them on all sides. They touched the smooth hard surfaces of the tapering pillars, and gazed upward in awe at the domed ceiling with its elaborate array of hanging formations.

They had almost reached the center of the vast chamber when suddenly they stopped, clutching each other in panic. Someone had shouted. The cry, short and sharp and very near, struck them like a blow, and then was gone—only to return in a hundred chattering echoes. A moment later the cavern was alive with motion as human figures emerged from behind every pillar and boulder and moved swiftly towards them.

They seemed to be everywhere—dozens of swarthy men and women, dressed in tight-fitting fur tunics. And in their hands, thrust forward before them, or brandished threateningly over their heads, were strange shiny objects—lengths of metal, thick and heavy and blunt-ended, or long and slender and sharply edged and tipped.

CHAPTER SIXTEEN

That day, the second day of the seventh moon, had been a time of strange and unprecedented happenings. Early in the morning there had been the departure of two Olzhaan on a journey that would take them below the Root, toward midday two children had been abducted from their nid-place, and in the early afternoon a threat had been made—a threat of violence. In the early evening the soft, flower-sweet breeze that breathed constantly through the forest heights died away to nothing, and a strange unaccustomed hush fell over Orbora. A misty haze rose up from fern-choked depths, and the last rays of the sinking sun faded into long pallid fingers of ghostly light. In the last hour of sunlight, Raamo left the palace of D'ol Falla and made his way across the central platform of Temple Grove, through a world turned alien and unfamiliar. He was on his way to the palace of the novice-master.

Raamo had no wish to see D'ol Regle or to speak to him. The thought of looking into his eyes was painful almost beyond enduring. But D'ol Falla was weak and ill, and there was no one else to carry the message. Waiting for admittance at the entryway to the palace of the novice-master, Raamo's mind was in such turmoil that he was not sure he would remember all that should be said—or, indeed, if he would be able to speak at all.

At last a Kindar serving man appeared and let Raamo into the palace. The serving man was tall and stoop shouldered with blunt unlined features and shallow eyes, and he stared at Raamo strangely before he spoke.

"Greetings, D'ol Raamo," he said at last. "If you will follow me, I will take you to the reception hall where you can wait while I announce your presence to the novice-master."

When Raamo was seated on an ornate settee in the large reception hall, the serving man still lingered, staring. "My name is Pino," he said. "Pino D'erl."

"Greetings, Pino," Raamo said. "Do I know you? Have we met before?"

"No," the man said. He paused again and his smile was so strangely self-concious that Raamo, for a brief moment, tore his mind away from its painful musings and centered it on pensing. The man was mind-blocking, of course, but carelessly, and Raamo was able to pense an odd, feverish pridefulness. "No," the man repeated. "You do not know me yet, but I think you may know of me someday soon, and you might want to know that you have met me."

Puzzled, and too distracted by thoughts of his mission to lend his mind fully to the meaning of the serving man's strange demeanor, Raamo only nodded. "I thank you, Pino D'erl," he said. "May I ask that you announce me to the novice-master? It is important that I speak with him immediately."

The serving man left then, and returned shortly to say that D'ol Regle was awaiting D'ol Raamo in his chambers.

"If you will come with me," Pino D'erl said, and he led the way through chambers and hallways and up several rampways to the higher levels of the palace.

When they reached the private suite of the novice-master, a flight of beautifully constructed chambers suspended and cantilevered amid an intricate webbing of Vine and tendril, they found D'ol Regle awaiting them. He was seated in a large hanging chair, among dozens of large down-filled pillows. Dismissing the serving man with a wave of his hand, he leaned back among his billowing pillows, and regarded Raamo intently from beneath half-lowered eyelids.

Trembling, Raamo stared at the familiar face of the man he had seen almost daily for many months, but who now seemed mysteriously and terribly altered. The differences were intangible, nameless—the face not so much changed in line or expression as in rigidity and tone—as if it had set and hardened and in doing so had been transformed into something grossly sinister. Forgetting for the moment his own fear and anguish, Raamo focused his mind on seeking out what lay behind the flushed face and majestic calm of the novice-master. D'ol Regle was, of course mind-blocking carefully, but Raamo could sense strain and a fleeting whisper of strong emotions. Centering his entire being and the full power of his Spirit-force on pensing, Raamo reached out —and found himself caught up in a strange current of unknown and unfamiliar power.

It was unlike anything he had ever before experienced —a wave, a current of immense impelling force in which his own Spirit joined, and for a moment was carried—lifted—soared. There was a great and joyful exhilaration and a feeling of strength and union and freedom, all in one. And then suddenly it was gone, and he was left behind.

Raamo looked around, frantically searching for the source of the strange power. It had not come from D'ol Regle, of that he was certain. It had seemed to have come from a place above and beyond—and yet, above this high-hung flight of the novice-master's palace, there would be nothing but the bare branched far-heights of the grunds, and the spreading fronds of roof-trees.

"What message have you brought me? Where is D'ol Falla?" The novice-master was staring at Raamo strangely. "What's the matter with you, D'ol Raamo? Are you ill, or have you, perhaps, gone mad?" D'ol Regle smiled sharply. "Or perhaps I should say, more completely mad than you and your accomplices have already shown yourselves to be."

Raamo turned his mind to D'ol Regle and his question with great reluctance.

"D'ol Falla is ill and very tired," he said. "She has sent me to tell you of our decision and to make a request." He paused, looking around him, as his mind turned again to the strange force—the current of power.

"Yes, yes?" D'ol Regle was saying impatiently. "And what is this decision?"

"D'ol Falla and I will do as you ask until D'ol Neric and D'ol Genaa return from below the Root. We will speak to no one of the Geets-kel or the true nature of the Pash-shan. And when the others return, we will tell them of your demands and we will then appear before you and the members of the Geets-kel in the secret meeting chamber as you have requested. But we can not promise for the others, for D'ol Neric and D'ol Genaa or for Hiro D'anhk whom they have gone to bring back from Erda. We can only promise that no one will be told until after we meet with you and the Geets-kel."

"And what is your request?"

"We don't know how long it will be—we think it may be several days before Neric and Genaa return from Erda. We ask that during that time the children, Pomma and Teera, be treated gently—that they not be frightened or—"

"Your request is granted," D'ol Regle interrupted. "The two children are being held in a secret place, but they are, and will be treated kindly—*unless* you forget your promise."

Again the threat. Although Raamo had heard of it from D'ol Falla, although he knew beyond the faintest doubt that D'ol Falla had recounted it truly and accurately, he had not, himself, heard the words spoken. He had not heard D'ol Regle, novice-master and Ol-zhaan of great fame and honor, speak words of violence against children. And, thus, there had remained some feeling of unreality—an insulating distance, between Raamo and the full meaning of the threat.

But hearing it now, he was suddenly sickened. A bitter revulsion made him turn away, and extending his arms as if to ward off an evil dream, he stumbled towards the chamber door. Behind him, D'ol Regle blew sharply on a signal flute, and the serving man, Pino D'erl, appeared in the doorway. Raamo quickly followed him from the room.

Just outside the doorway, Raamo paused and breathed deeply of the fresh untainted air. And it was then that the feeling came again. More distant and fleeting this time, but just as infinitely engrossing, it caught him up for a brief moment and made him a part of its overwhelming power. And then it was gone, and Raamo was left to follow the still strangely smirking serving-man to the palace dooryard.

The sun was gone, and as Raamo made his way back across the central platform and up the branchway that led to the Novice Hall, the first slow drops of the night rain had begun to fall. Lifting his face to the rain, Raamo wondered why he had never before thought that the soft warm drops of the first rain were very much like tears.

On the next morning and the one that followed, Raamo followed his regular schedule as a novice Ol-zhaan assigned to future service as a priest of the Vine. Just as before, he spent the morning hours in the palace of the High-priest, and as before, much of that time was spent in discourse with D'ol Falla. But now D'ol Falla spoke of many things other than the ancient rituals of the Ceremonies of the Vine. All during the long hours of those mornings while they awaited the return of Neric and Genaa, Raamo and D'ol Falla spoke of many, many things, and Raamo learned much that he had not known before.

During her many years of study of the books and records of the Forgotten, D'ol Falla had discovered many facts about the past. She knew much about the long centuries before the Flight, about the Flight itself, and of the early years on the planet of Green-sky. She spoke to Raamo of all these things, but in particular she spoke of the man called Nesh-om and of his dreams for the Kindar and for the future of Green-sky.

"It was in his early youth, long before the Flight that D'ol Nesh-om began his studies," she told Raamo. "Unlike many thinkers of his time, he did not believe that human beings were instinctively violent. He felt that if violence had at one time been instinctive, it had been unproductive for many centuries and would long since have disappeared if it were not for the human institutions that depended on, and fostered, violent and competitive behavior. D'ol Nesh-om's early writings were full of observations concerning the philosophies and institutions of that time—institutions that to you, Raamo, or to any citizen of Green-sky, would seem incredibly foolish and evil.

There were in those days, for instance, strange taboos that made many forms of behavior that arose from feelings of Love and close human communion inappropriate or even obscene, while expressions of aggression and anger were permitted and even, at times, admired. Children were carefully prevented from experiencing the Joys of many forms of close human contact, while being permitted, even encouraged, to attend events—games and diversions—that glorified violent and aggressive behavior.

But then came the Flight, and a chance for D'ol Nesh-om to test his theories by planning and setting up new institutions that would encourage the development of the highest human potentials. Under his guidance all the institutions of Green-sky were planned and organized—from those concerned with the production and distribution of goods to the ones that structured domestic life and the nurturing of future generations. But the first purpose of every institution was to satisfy every natural human drive in such a way that the relationship of those satisfactions to the highest of all human needs was constantly reaffirmed and emphasized. Through ritual and ceremony, every need was related to the holy needs of the Spirit—the yearning for Love and Spirit-oneness. And as the years passed and the first generation of Kindar grew to maturity, D'ol Nesh-om's hopes were justified, again and again. New forces of Spirit, some even that D'ol Nesh-om himself had not foreseen, were evolving and developing. Life in Green-sky was becoming daily, not only more serene and joyous, but also more full of portents and omens of great new changes yet to come. It was not, in fact, until that last decade of D'ol Nesh-om's life, that the phenomenon of uniforce began to play a significant part in the lives of the people.

"It would have been wonderful to have lived then—in those days," Raamo mused, "when it was possible to take part in uniforce. I have often thought of it and wondered what it would have been like."

"There are accounts in the old records," D'ol Falla said. "But it was a great mystery, even then. No one learned to teach it—because it was a learning that did not depend on what lay within the power of the individual mind. But when it occurred it seemed infinite, of infinite potential and power."

D'ol Falla's face, which had been enlivened by the enthusiasm she felt for the work of D'ol Nesh-om, grew somber, and the delicate traceries of age once more formed patterns of weariness and anxiety. "But then came the great controversy, between D'ol Nesh-om and D'ol Wissen," she said.

Raamo had heard before of the debate between the two great leaders, from D'ol Falla, and also, in a brief and inaccurate form in the lectures of D'ol Regle. But he had never been able to grasp just why the disagreement had assumed such great significance.

"But I don't understand why D'ol Wissen felt it was

so necessary to keep the knowledge of the past—of the destruction of the ancestral planet—from the Kindar," he told D'ol Falla.

D'ol Wissen believed that there was in human nature a deep instinctive need for violent and passionate behavior—a demonic force. He felt it would rise up from time to time, not only in individuals but in civilizations as well. He was sure that it was necessary to suppress not only every violent instinct, but also all knowledge of the possibility of violence. This, of course, meant that it was necessary to perpetuate the division of society into Kindar and Ol-zhaan—that there should always be a small group, an elite, armed with the knowledge of the past, who would, alone, be able to guard against the return of its evils.

But D'ol Nesh-om did not agree. He felt that the force D'ol Wissen feared was not the result of a need for violence, but only a need for intensity—for intensity of feeling and emotion—for passionate involvement of both mind and Spirit. Having achieved this involvement in positive, affirming relationships, the Kindar would be free forever from the ancient demons of their violent past.

But D'ol Nesh-om died, and D'ol Wissen triumphed," D'ol Falla said. "And now, Raamo, we are facing again the dilemma faced in the old world by those who believed that violence was evil. We must decide as they were forced to do, whether to submit to evil, or to use evil methods to oppose it."

When D'ol Falla returned to the question of an answer to violence, as she did many times, Raamo could only shake his head. He knew what she was seeking. It was true that he had, in the past, seen visions, visions that were, perhaps, foretellings. But he had never been certain that they were true foretellings. And what did seem very certain was that he was not able to summon a foretelling at will.

"I have tried and tried, D'ol Falla," he told her. "Most often I hear nothing at all. But when I try the hardest—when I reach out until I am exhausted—" he paused, and then continued reluctantly. "When you first asked me to seek for an answer, the words of a song came to my mind—a nonsense verse sung in a game of children. And now, when I seek for a foretelling, the words of the song keep returning, filling my mind until they drown out all other thought or feeling." Looking into D'ol Falla's eyes, he let her read his frustration and regret. "A nonsense song of children," he repeated ruefully.

CHAPTER SEVENTEEN

Transfixed with fright, Genaa and Neric stood in helpless silence while all around them the Erdlings moved forward. They came slowly, holding their tools of violence between them and their quarry, and when at last the circle had grown so small that they stood almost shoulder to shoulder, they came to a stop.

It was not until then that Neric, emerging from the blind paralysis of terror, began to realize that the threat expressed by the brandished weapons was not fully reflected in the faces that surrounded him. Looking into the fixed and staring eyes of the Erdlings, he began to be aware that he and Genaa were surrounded by fear and uncertainty, as well as aggression.

Very slowly, he began to lift his hands. As he did so, those Erdlings directly in front of him shrank back in fear, and a threatening murmur arose from behind him. But when his arms were fully extended in the Kindar gesture of welcome and greeting, the murmur faded—and at last he found his voice.

"Greetings, friend, and welcome," his voice quavered, and as he spoke he became aware that Genaa was speaking with him. Glancing at her he saw that she too was making the sign of welcome.

"We come in Peace." It was Genaa who spoke now. "We come on a mission of friendship to the leaders of the Erdlings."

"What do you want?" It was an Erdling who spoke, a stocky, bushy-haired man, who stood directly in front of Neric. His speech, like Teera's, seemed slurred and drawling. "It is not to be believed that Ol-zhaan come offering friendship," he said.

"But we do," Genaa said. "Truly. We wish only good for the Erdlings—and for their freedom."

The gasp of shocked disbelief came in unison from many throats. Glancing at Genaa, Neric saw that she was smiling—that dazzling, insidious smile capable of robbing the mind of all logic and reason. Often in the past Neric had resented the power of that smile, but now he could not have been more glad for it. It was easy to see that even Erdlings were not immune to its charm. The bushy-haired man, who seemed to be looked to as a leader by the others, was allowing the arm that bore his weapon to sink slowly to his side.

"What, then, do you wish?" he said, uncertainly.

"We wish to speak to the members of your Council, and in particular to the Verban known as Hiro D'anhk," Neric said.

"We would be most grateful if you would—" Genaa was saying when her voice suddenly faltered. Neric looked and saw that she was deathly pale. Putting her hands to her face, she staggered backwards. Weapons clattered to the earth as Erdling hands shot out in quick response before she could fall. It was not until then that Neric realized that he, too, was weak and ill, and very near to fainting. Sinking to his knees, he waited until the whirling darkness that had seemed to be closing in around him began to lighten.

"What is it?" an Erdling voice asked. "What is wrong?"

"I don't know," Neric said. "Except we have been lost in the tunnels for a long time. We have been long without food or rest. And then the sudden shock—" he gestured around him, smiling weakly, "—of your reception—"

"Food!" the bushy-haired man bellowed suddenly. "Is there any food among us?"

There was a sudden bustle of conversation, but no food seemed to be forthcoming.

"No one seems to be carrying food on their person," the bushy-haired man said, "but it is not far to the southern factories. We will send runners. They will be back very soon with some food from the midday rations. In the meantime we will rest here."

A dozen Erdling hands supported Neric as he sank back to the sandy floor of the cavern, where Genaa was already resting, and in a moment the entire group of Erdlings closed in around them in a close packed circle. Neric saw that there were not as many as he had thought at first—not the hundreds they had seemed when they had appeared as an advancing army of weapon bearers. As they gathered around him now, he could see that there were no more than thirty, among whom were men and women of varying ages, and of widely differing appearance.

For a long moment there was silence as thirty pairs of eyes stared at Neric and Genaa with avid interest. A hand reached out tentatively, and fingers touched the silken material of Genaa's shuba. There was a soft gasp of appreciative wonder, and then many hands stretched forward, to touch her shuba and Neric's also. Then the silence returned.

After a time the bushy-haired man made a rasping sound in his throat in preparation for speaking. Everyone turned to him as he said, "My name is Rad Arba. I am the foreman of the casting caves in the bronze works. And these others," he gestured around him, "are all members of my crew—except for those two, who are plak hunters. I would like to welcome you, for myself and these others, to Erda."

"We thank you," Neric said. "We are very thankful for your welcome. May I ask, Rad Arba, how you happened to be here in this cavern—awaiting us?"

"It was the hunters who found you," Rad Arba said. "We were at work in the casting cave, little more than an hour ago, when these two burst in upon us from the southern tunnels, crying that they had seen two Ol-zhaan not far away in an abandoned rail tunnel. There seemed to be no time to assemble the Council and ask their advice, so we armed ourselves with hammers and chisels and came here to the cavern of the three lakes and waited."

Then another among the Erdlings spoke, a woman this time. "You spoke of freedom for the Erdlings," she said. "Do the Ol-zhaan truly wish the Erdlings to be free?"

"There are some among the Ol-zhaan who believe the Erdlings should be released," Neric said. "But there are others who do not agree. That is why we have come to Erda; to confer with the leaders of the Erdlings to determine how we can convince all the Ol-zhaan that no evil would come from the release of the people of Erda."

"How can we be freed?" the woman asked. "Will the Root shrink away?"

Neric glanced at Genaa. "There are things we must wait to speak of until we have met with your Council," Genaa said quickly. "Their advice will be needed in the solution of many problems. When we have spoken with the Council, many questions can be answered."

"How far are we from your city?" Neric asked. "Will it take us long to reach it?"

"Our factory is one of the most distant from the Center," Rad said. "It takes half an hour by rail car and then almost as long on foot to reach the Center and the Council Cavern. But if you go dressed like that—in the garments of Ol-zhaan—it may take much longer, if you reach it at all."

"What is your advice, then, Rad Arba?" Neric asked. "What can we do to reach your Councilors quickly and without confusion or delay?"

On being asked to take responsibility for the transportation of the Ol-zhaan to the Center of Erda, the Erdling factory foreman became suddenly wary. Frowning, he shook his bushy head. "I cannot say," he said. "It is one thing for me to find your story acceptable to my reason, but who can say that I am wise enough to judge truly. If your story is false and you mean harm to the people of Erda, I would not wish to be responsible."

Stepping forward, Neric held out his hands, palms outward. "Here," he said, "I have heard that most Erdlings can pense emotions. Perhaps you can pense my true feeling towards the people of Erda."

For only a moment the foreman hesitated; but then, looking around him at the eager faces of his fellow workers, he too stepped forward, and thrust out his hands. The cavern became very quiet as Neric placed his palms on those of Rad Arba and stared into his eyes. For what seemed a very long time the two men, Ol-zhaan and Erdling, stood very still while Genaa and the Erdling bronze workers watched in almost breathless silence. At last Rad Arba drew away, shaking his head slowly. Turning to his crew he shrugged, smiling ruefully.

"Who would have dreamed of pensing an Ol-zhaan?" he said. And then to Neric, "I will take you and the woman Ol-zhaan to the Council."

Not long afterwards Genaa and Neric set out again on their journey. Somewhat refreshed by their brief rest and by the food provided by Rad's messengers, they were led out of the cavern and through a series of well-lit tunnels. They had not gone far when they became aware of strange smells and noises, and were shortly led into a small cavern full of weird and fantastic sights and sounds.

Smoking pits of thick glowing liquids, stone tables covered with strange objects shaped of richly gleaming materials, strange clanging noises and harsh acrid smells—this was Rad Arba's casting cavern and the work-place of his crew of Erdlings. While Neric and Genaa stared with wonder, the foreman chose three of his crew to accompany him and the Ol-zhaan to the Center. Then as the rest of his crew gathered around the Ol-zhaan to bid them farewell, he carefully instructed them to guard their loose Erdling tongues, and to speak to no one of what they had just witnessed, at least, until such time as he, himself, returned and relieved them of their pledge of silence.

So Neric and Genaa accomplished the final portion of their journey carefully draped in long robes of lapan skin and escorted by four Erdlings. But even with all that marked them as Ol-zhaan hidden from view, they continued to arouse much interest and curiosity as they made their way through the outskirts of Erda. Their unfamiliar faces, as well as their cropped hair and Kindar pallor, caused them to be identified as newly rescued Verban—and therefore the objects of great curiosity and sympathetic interest. Time and time again it was necessary for Rad Arba and his three fellow bronze workers to discourage the advances of the Erdlings—men, women and even children who approached wishing to speak to the newly arrived Verban.

"They are ill and exhausted," he told the would-be well-wishers. "We are taking them to the Council. There will be time enough to greet them later."

Overwhelmed by the strangeness of their surroundings, Neric and Genaa were immensely grateful for the protection and guidance of their escorts. Carried rapidly through tunnels lit by blazing wall-torches, in a clattering basket-shaped rail car, and then led down crowded passageways among crowds of fur-clad strangers, and finally escorted through enormous caverns divided into many chambers by stone walls and metal partitions, they at last reached the great cavern that contained the Council Chambers. There they waited while the Councilors were notified, and while Rad Arba, himself, continued to the Academy to summon Hiro D'anhk.

The Councilors assembled in a small conference chamber just off the great assembly cavern, and there Neric and Genaa were presented to them and began to try to tell their story. It was obvious, however, that the Councilors had not yet had time to recover from their shocked confusion at finding themselves in the presence of Ol-zhaan. Little communication had been accomplished when the chamber door was thrown open and the Verban, Hiro D'anhk, strode into the room.

But if the sudden appearance in Erda—in their own conference chamber—of two young strangers clad in the garments of Ol-zhaan was almost beyond comprehension to the Councilors, what happened next was not. As they watched the meeting between father and daughter, their fear and confusion was swept away with what seemed to Neric to be amazing suddenness. As Neric watched, the smiles and tears of Genaa and Hiro D'anhk appeared like reflections in a gazing bowl on the faces of the Councilors. Minutes passed, with Genaa and her father still engrossed in their greeting; and the Erdlings seemingly quite content to share their Joy—oblivious to all other considerations. At last Neric decided to act. Rising, he stepped forward, clearing his throat.

There was much to be done. There was much that had to be explained to the Councilors, and as Neric began the explanations, Genaa at last left her father's arms and joined in the telling. They spoke to the Erdling Councilors of the Geets-kel, the secret inner group of Ol-zhaan, who, alone over the years, had known the secret of the true nature of the people of Erda, and who were responsible for their imprisonment. They explained the delicate and dangerous position of the few who opposed the Geets-kel; of the need to prepare the Kindar as well as the majority of the Ol-zhaan that they might accept the release of the Erdlings. And they pleaded for permission to take Hiro D'anhk to Orbora to confirm the claims of the rebels. Along with this, they tried to make clear the danger of the too-sudden release of the people of Erda before the Kindar learned the truth—and finally, of the need for haste.

Speaking in turns, Neric and Genaa and even at

times, Hiro D'anhk, went over and over the explanations. At times Neric grew impatient, forgetting for the moment the unthinkable nature of their revelations to Erdling minds. It was not that the Erdlings found it hard to grasp the meaning of their words. Their difficulty seemed to lie in reacting to those meanings. To relate to Ol-zhaan as human beings—as fallible and changeable members of humanity, rather than as superhuman creatures of inevitable cruelty—required an adjustment that could not be quickly or easily accomplished.

At last Kir Oblan, the Chief Councilor, indicated that the Council understood and approved the goals of the rebel Ol-zhaan and were willing to cooperate with them. "What is it that you wish us to do?" he asked.

It was Genaa who answered, "We wish to be supplied with food and lanterns and to be taken, with my father, Hiro D'anhk, to the cavern where we met Rad Arba and his workers. From there we will be able to return to Orbora. And if we are successful we will soon return with many other Ol-zhaan and Kindar to begin the process that will set the people of Erda free."

"And if you fail?" Kir Oblan asked.

"If we fail," Neric said, "the people of Erda will be no worse off than they are now—but you will hear no more of us."

Speaking in low voices the Councilors conferred for what seemed an endless length of time before they again addressed the Ol-zhaan.

"Your request is granted," Kir Oblan then announced. "In two hours, at the time of the evening food-taking, when there will be the fewest Erdlings in the public tunnels, we will allow Rad Arba to take you back to the cavern where he first found you. In taking this action, we are breaking the laws that govern this Council, which state that all matters of importance be discussed in open council in the great cavern before the people of Erda. It is true that this is a matter of great importance, which may affect the lives of all Erdlings. But it seems to be true also that there is need for haste and that the success of your plan depends on your early return to Green-sky. And, as Hiro D'anhk can tell you, it is not easy to quickly resolve even matters of small importance, in Erda. Therefore it is of the utmost importance that you leave Erda as quickly and as secretly as possible."

At that moment, Kir Oblan was interrupted by a loud metallic pounding which seemed to come from the door to the chamber, and at almost the same moment an Erdling, a young man with a red face and a breathless, agitated manner, burst into the room. Standing with his back against the door he glanced rather wildly about the room.

"What is it, Tral?" the chief Councilor asked. "Why have you intruded on our conference?"

"I have been sent as a messenger—from those who await you in the great cavern—in the assembly hall."

"Who is it that awaits us there?" Kir Oblan asked.

"The people. The people of Erda. They have gathered in the great cavern to take part in the Council concerning—" The young man paused and glanced nervously around the chamber, and his eyes, falling on Neric and Genaa, became fixed and rigid, and for some seconds he said nothing at all. At last, swallowing with obvious difficulty he went on "—concerning the captured Olzhaan," he whispered huskily.

CHAPTER EIGHTEEN

Soon after the messenger burst into the conference chamber, Neric and Genaa, stripped of their camouflage of lapan fur, were led out onto the platform in the great assembly cavern, before an immense gathering of Erdlings. There was, Kir Oblan had said, no longer any choice.

"But how did they learn of our presence in Erda?" Neric asked when the messenger had finished speaking. "Who betrayed us?"

"I don't know that it was a matter of betrayal," Kir Oblan said. "But there were many who knew—all those in Rad's crew—and secrets fare badly in Erda. Could it be, Rad, that your people are responsible?"

The foreman shrugged. "It is quite possible," he said. "I told them not to speak of it, but the temptation would have been very great. I am sure they meant no harm. Without doubt someone told a few, pledging them to silence, and each of those told a few others, and on and on— You know how such things happen, Councilor."

"What will happen now?" Genaa asked.

"You will have to go before the people and tell them your story as you have told us," Kir Oblan said. "Then, if it is the will of the people, you will be free to go."

"But you said it would take a long time," Neric said.

Kir Oblan sighted. "True," he said. "I did. And I'm afraid that it will. It may take a very long time, indeed. But I'm afraid that there is no other choice."

And so the two Ol-zhaan were led forth, accompanied by Hiro D'anhk, and when the people of Erda saw them and their gleaming robes, a strange sound rose from the huge crowd—a low ominous moan that seemed to come from one enormous throat.

Striding forward, Kir Oblan began to speak, but he had gotten no further than, "People of Erda," when a noisy commotion broke out far back in the cavern as a group of Erdlings rose and began to make their way to the platform. They were led by a short man with earth-hued skin, who pushed his way roughly through the crowd, brandishing a pointed length of metal over his head and shouting, "Death to the Ol-zhaan! Death to the enemy of Erda."

"Go back, Befal," Kir Oblan shouted. "Go back and await your turn to address the Council."

But Axon Befal and the mob of Nekom continued to press forward until they were within a few feet of the platform edge. But at that moment another voice was heard clearly over the noise of the crowd.

"Stay where you are, Axon Befal," the voice said and the leader of the Nekom looked up into the face of the Verban, Hiro D'anhk.

The tall Verban had advanced suddenly to stand beside Kir Oblan at the edge of the platform, and there was that in his voice that caused a sudden hush to fall over the great cavern. Even Befal, himself, seemed to be momentarily struck dumb. The last faint echoes of turmoil whispered away into silence as all eyes turned to

the vivid face of the exiled Kindar.

"People of Erda," Hiro D'anhk's crisp Kindar voice rang out. "Have you come here to listen to the Nekom's old and deadly dream, or would you hear a dream of hope? Hope for the people of Erda as well as for those who dwell in Green-sky. If you would choose hope you must listen—to me and to these young Ol-zhaan. You must hear that there are some among the Ol-zhaan who are convinced that the people of Erda must be set free."

A gasp of wonder and disbelief spread through the cavern, and as Hiro D'anhk waited for it to fade, Axon Befal suddenly recovered his voice. "Who are you Verban, homeless one, to give advice to the people of Erda?" he shouted.

"And who are the Nekom to speak for all the people of Erda?" Hiro D'anhk's voice rang out into a shocked silence. "Why should the life-loving people of Erda allow themselves to be led by the few among them who have devoted themselves to death and vengeance. Why should those few be heard above all others only because they shout more loudly than those who speak with Love and wisdom?"

A murmur spread through the cavern, and when Axon Befal vaulted onto the platform a moment later and began to shout, the murmur grew into a roar.

"Be silent, Befal! Wait your turn to speak. Let the Ol-zhaan be heard," the Erdlings shouted, and continued to shout until the leader of the Nekom had relinquished his place on the platform and returned to the cavern floor.

As Kir Oblan had warned, it was not to be done quickly. There was, first of all, the story to be told again —in great detail. Speaking in turns, Neric and Genaa, and Hiro as well, told the Erdlings of the Geets-kel and their secrets, and of the rebel Ol-zhaan. They spoke of the need for Hiro D'anhk to return to Orbora to bear witness to the true nature of those who were called the Pash-shan. They spoke of the dangers, and of the need for haste. And they spoke long and carefully of the danger to both Kindar and Erdling, if the Erdlings were too quickly released into Green-sky, before the Kindar were prepared for their coming.

Several times during the telling of the story, the leader of the Nekom made new attempts to gain the attention of the audience, but each time he was shouted into silence. At last he changed his tactics and, with his followers imitating him, he began to shout meaningless noises, intent only in drowning out the voices of the speakers. For a few minutes this new tactic seemed to be successful—if the Nekom were not allowed to speak, no one else would be. But then the crowd around the clump of Nekom began to surge forward, working their way in among the followers of Befal and opening the way for other infiltrators who came after them. And when the shouters found themselves surrounded, not by fellow Nekom, but by others, who stared at them silently, the shouts dwindled into stillness.

But when the Ol-zhaan had finished speaking and their story had been told it was, by Erdling custom, the time to admit speakers from the audience; and many came forward to take their turn on the platform. Some wished to state their conviction that the two young Ol-zhaan spoke sincerely and from the truth at least as they knew it. A few even claimed to have pensed it, but there were many who had doubts and questions.

Among those who came forward was, of course, Axon Befal, and for his allotted time he was listened to by most of the huge gathering with interest but little enthusiasm. But when he had used up his time in confused demands for immediate release for all Erdlings and immediate execution of the two captive Ol-zhaan, he was once more shouted into silence.

The fierce ravings of Befal was soon followed by the calm but quavering voice of the old man, Vatar, the leader of the mystical society of Gystig. Stretching out his arms, the old man spoke to his fellow Erdlings of faith and humility and implored them not to put their hopes in the strangers who came offering a spurious freedom of the body.

When, at long last, no other came forward to claim their right to speak, Kir Oblan returned once more to the front of the platform.

"Having heard the suggestions of the people," he said, "we of the Council have a suggestion to offer for your approval. Although we see the wisdom in waiting until the Kindar have been prepared for our coming, and therefore in not insisting on the immediate destruction of the Root, we also understand the reasoning of those who are reluctant to allow these Ol-zhaan to depart with no assurance that they will remember their promises to the people of Erda. We therefore suggest that the two Ol-zhaan be allowed to depart with the Verban, Hiro D'anhk, but that they be required to take with them two or three Erdling representatives. Thus we can be more certain that our story will be well told and our cause well defended."

There was a murmur of approval as, all over the cavern, the Erdlings gestured their support of the Council's decision; and Kir Oblan turned to Neric and Genaa for their response.

"We have no objection," Genaa said. "Except that

whomever is chosen must be willing to share the risks of our mission. We do not know what our fate will be if we fail and the Geets-kel triumph. In the past, those whom the Geets-kel saw as threats to their power were imprisoned below the Root, and we do not know what else they might do—to what lengths they might go. So those who go with us must know that they go into danger."

Then, while Kir Oblan again addressed the assembly concerning the choosing of representatives, Neric and Genaa were taken back to the small conference room. There, at the insistence of Hiro D'anhk, they were supplied with nids of lapan fur.

"You must rest," Hiro said. "If only for an hour. It will not help your cause if you collapse from exhaustion in the tunnels. It will take a little time for the Council to choose the representatives and to collect the food and lanterns for our journey. Meanwhile, you must sleep."

Some time later Neric and Genaa were awakened from the deep sleep of complete exhaustion to find themselves surrounded by many people. There were the Councilors and Hiro, the foreman, Rad Arba, and two strangers, a man and a woman—the newly chosen Erdling ambassadors to Green-sky. There was much haste and confusion. Introductions were made, good-bys were said, and the journey begun, before the two Ol-zhaan had fully recovered from the effects of their deep slumber.

Walking swiftly, they had passed through several small chambers and dimly lit tunnels before Neric realized that they were being led by half a dozen Erdlings, wearing bronze insignia on their chests.

"Who are they? Why are they with us?" he asked Hiro D'anhk.

"They are wardens," Hiro said. "They will escort us as

far as the cavern of three lakes, and then remain there when we have gone on to see that we are not followed. The Councilors felt it was necessary."

"It is necessary. We are certain to be followed by many, out of curiosity, if not for more sinister reasons." It was one of the Erdling representatives who spoke—the man—tall for an Erdling with deep-set, darkly shadowed eyes.

Neric turned to the speaker. "You are, then, one of those chosen to accompany us to Green-sky?" Neric asked. "I am sorry, but I was only half-awake when you were named to me. Your name is—?"

"I am Herd Eld," the man said. "The father of the child, Teera. And this," he indicated the woman who walked beside him, "is her mother, my bond-partner, Kanna."

"Teera's parents," Neric gasped. "Genaa, did you know this?"

Genaa, who was walking just ahead, turned back. "Yes," she said. "I guessed it when I heard their names. But I thought it wise to say nothing before the Councilors, since we had not spoken to them of Teera earlier." And then, speaking to Herd and Kanna she said, "We had agreed not to mention Teera to the Councilors since her presence in Green-sky has little bearing on our mission and would only have caused further lengthy discussions."

Herd nodded. "The hunter, Tocar, who brought us word that Teera was alive and in Green-sky, warned us to say nothing of what we had learned. And the Councilors chose us from among the volunteers for other reasons—perhaps because we had few to grieve for us if we did not return. But you were wise to keep silent. If they had learned that Teera was in Green-sky, there would have had to be endless explanations. And it is quite possible that the Councilors would have decided that ambassadors with less complicated motives would have served better."

"Have you seen Teera recently?" Kanna asked. "Is she well?"

"She was very well when we last saw her," Genaa said. "That was on the day that Tocar was sent to you with news of her."

At that moment the Erdling escorts came to a stop before a heavy door, and one of their number turned to speak.

"Beyond this point," he said, "we must go by way of the public areas. They will be crowded. No doubt many who would ordinarily be in their own clancaverns for the evening food-taking at this hour will be waiting in the public passageways, hoping for a glimpse of the Ol-zhaan. Most will be only curious, but as you witnessed in the great cavern, there are some among us whose minds have been poisoned by hatred. The Councilors felt that there might be danger. Therefore we will walk swiftly, surrounding the two Ol-zhaan so that they may not be closely approached by anyone from the crowd. When we reach the rails, a car will be waiting for us."

The double doors swung open into a huge shop cavern. Here and there in front of the various stalls, were groups of Erdlings engaged in animated conversation. But they fell instantly silent as they became aware of the Ol-zhaan. From all sides they pressed forward, surrounding the small caravan. Falling back before the waving arms of the wardens, they immediately closed in behind and followed. As the procession passed through tunnels and caverns, their numbers grew until it seemed to Neric, glancing back, that a dark, moving forest of humanity stretched behind them. A forest that moved forward so relentlessly that it seemed it might, overtaking its quarry, sweep over it, trampling it into the dusty earth.

The caravan had formed itself into a tight pattern. First Rad Arba, then two of the Erdling escorts and Hiro D'anhk, then Neric and Genaa flanked on each side by Kanna and Herd Eld, and then the remaining escorts. And behind them, pressing closer and closer, a thousand Erdlings straining to draw near enough to see the Ol-zhaan—or, perhaps, to do more.

In the narrowest tunnels, Erdlings meeting the caravan were forced to step back to the walls to let it pass. However, because of the narrow space, they remained almost within arm's reach of the Ol-zhaan. Down these corridors, closely lined with faces, alight with avid interest, Neric and Genaa walked in fear, remembering the burning eyes and brandished weapons of the Nekom.

Too frightened and agitated to focus his Spirit-force, Neric was unable, even in the close-packed tunnels, to pense more than an ill-defined excited and fearful interest from the Erdlings that pressed in around him. But once or twice he was startled by a fleeting impression of something else, something harsh and bitter, and as shocking as sudden pain.

At last the caravan reached the beginning of the rail lines; and there most of the followers were left behind. A single car awaited them at the loading platform, and only the members of their party were allowed to board. As the car moved forward, Neric sighed with relief, but a few moments later, he noticed Herd Eld speaking urgently to Hiro D'anhk. Then Hiro turned to Neric.

"Herd thinks it might be wise for you and Genaa to move to the center of the car," he said. "We will soon be passing intersecting tunnels."

Once more aware of a heavy burden of anxiety, Neric moved with Genaa to the more protected area. But the intersections sped by without incident, and it was not long before the car came to a stop at the entrance of the southern factory caverns. Making their way past the nearly deserted caves of the bronze works, the caravan followed Rad Arba through a series of tunnels that led, at last, to the cavern of the three lakes. There were several openings where tunnels opened into the huge cavern, but Rad led the way unhesitatingly to one.

"It was here," he said, "that the Ol-zhaan appeared from the darkness."

And it was here that good-bys were said, as the foreman turned back and the six Erdling wardens prepared to remain behind to guard the mouth of the tunnel. Then, their lanterns lit and blazing, the five went on alone—the two Ol-zhaan, the Verban and the two Erdling ambassadors.

They moved quickly in the bright glow of the lanterns, and it was not long before Genaa discovered the first small spray of fern. Holding it up, withered and dusty, she suddenly laughed aloud. She had been dreading the return to the deserted tunnels; but now that they were there, it all seemed much less terrible. They had food and light, her father walked beside her, and the withered fern pointed the way back to Green-sky. But then, suddenly, Herd Eld put his hand across her mouth.

"Be silent," he said urgently.

"What is it?" Hiro whispered.

Herd pointed to the floor of the tunnel. Looking, Genaa saw loose soil, drifted dust and a length of half buried rail. "What is it?" she whispered.

"After Teera disappeared I spent many days in the tunnels," Herd spoke softly. "I learned to read the dust as one reads a printed slate. Many feet have passed this way, very recently."

"The Nekom?" Hiro guessed.

"Perhaps. If they guessed you might return the way you came, they could have bribed or tricked one of Rad's people into bringing them here. They may be planning to wait for us somewhere on ahead."

"What shall we do?" It was Kanna who broke the shocked silence.

"I have a plan," Herd said. "Just a few yards farther on there is a large ventilation tunnel. The four of you must climb up it to the end and wait; I will go on alone."

"But why Herd?" Kanna asked.

"I know these tunnels well. I can move quickly and quietly. Perhaps I can discover who it is and what may be their purpose. And if they are Nekom, I may be able to decoy them into taking a wrong turning."

It seemed a faint hope but, perhaps, the only one. So the others waited with extinguished lanterns in a small lookout chamber below the Root, while Herd went on alone. The time passed slowly. Hardly daring to whisper, they waited in silence, constantly listening for the sound of approaching footsteps. From time to time Kanna wept quietly, and the others embraced her in a silent sharing of her grief and fear.

After what seemed many hours, but could, perhaps, have been no more than one, there was the sudden sound of footsteps. The steps were slow and groping, and a moment later Herd crawled up the narrow tunnel. In the dim light that filtered down through the Root it was apparent that his face was tense and strained and that he no longer carried his lantern.

"Light your lanterns," he said. "We must go quickly. I'll tell you what happened later when we are beyond pursuit."

For a time they went quickly, without stopping to look for pieces of fern. "There is no need yet," Herd whispered. "You came this way, I know. There is a point farther on when we will have to watch again for your markers."

They went on, almost running. Several times the light from the lanterns revealed intersecting tunnels—tunnels of which Neric and Genaa had been entirely unaware when they had passed that way in total darkness. An one intersection Herd paused briefly and listened, and then hurried on. A few moments later he stopped and looked around.

"It was here," he said. "It was here that they turned back. From now on we must go carefully, disturbing the ground as little as possible and picking up every piece of fern."

They had gone on for more than an hour, passing many intersections, before Herd stopped again. "I think we are safe now, at least for a time. Let us stop here for a little."

They rested then and listened while Herd Eld told a strange tale of stalking the warlike Nekom—as the Nekom, themselves, stalked something or someone that was moving through the tunnels ahead of them. As he talked, Herd began to smile.

"It did not seem amusing at the time," he said. "I was

far too frightened to find it so. But when I picture it now—myself, creeping silently, with darkened lantern after a large group of Nekom, who were creeping silently after a quarry who seemed to be just ahead. Now and then Befal would give a signal—he alone was carrying a lighted lantern—and the Nekom would stop and listen; and then I could hear it, too. Something else was moving through the tunnels not far beyond.

"Then Befal decided it was time to charge. Suddenly the Nekom rushed forward into the darkness, and in a moment I heard screams of fright and the sounds of struggle. I arrived outside the ring of light from Befal's lantern in time to see the stately Bruha release herself from the grasp of several Nekom and pronounce an awesome litany of curses on all Nekom, and on Axon Befal in particular." Herd's smile grew broader. "The Nekom had been following a half-dozen Hax-dok, led by Bruha, herself."

"But how—?" Kanna said.

"Who knows. Perhaps the same enterprising bronze worker who led the Nekom to the tunnel earlier sold his services to the Hax-dok. Bruha had planned, no doubt, to witness the ritual by which our Ol-zhaan made possible our escape through the Root; and, having thus learned the secrets, she would return to Erda in triumph—where she would repeat the miracle—waiting, no doubt, only long enough for the Erdlings to offer her an appropriate amount of honor and power, in exchange for her magical services.

"At any rate, they argued mightily for some time—Bruha and Befal—shouting accusations; but at last Befal offered to allow the two Ol-zhaan to live long enough, after their capture, to teach Bruha their rituals.

It was then that I began to put my plan into action.

"I retreated a little way down the tunnel, lit my lantern and turned it very low. Drawing their attention by crying out as though in fright, I turned and ran. They came after me in a thundering herd, perhaps twenty Nekom and five or six Hax-dok. I turned at the first intersecting tunnel and ran up it until I passed a mass of grundroot protruding from the tunnel wall. A few yards farther on I smashed my lantern, as though it had been dropped in flight, and then I ran back and crouched against the root.

"They thundered past, stopping for a moment, to examine the lantern, and then running on at top speed. And then I crept back to where you were waiting."

Herd laughed then, unrestrainedly, and the others joined him, forgetting for the moment the trials and dangers that still lay ahead. For at least the tunnel before them was clear; the fern lay undisturbed marking the way; and somewhere ahead lay the secret opening and the forest of Green-sky.

CHAPTER NINETEEN

"How many days has it been?" Teera asked.

"Five, I think, or six," Pomma told her. "I'm not sure anymore. It seems like forever and—" She stopped, noticing that Teera was, once more, close to tears. It still frightened her to see Teera cry, even though she had long since learned that the weeping did not last for long and seemed to do Teera no lasting harm. In fact, she sometimes seemed to be the better for it.

There had been times, in the last few days, when Pomma had even thought of trying it herself. Of throwing herself on the floor in a frenzy of sobs and gasps and flooding tears—just to see what it would feel like. In fact, she had tried, allowing herself to think of her parents and their grief and of her own growing fear that she and Teera were to be imprisoned for the rest of their lives. But although she could sometimes feel her eyes grow hot and wet, the first loud sob usually shocked her into silence. She had been too well trained in Joy.

Now, running to Teera, she threw her arms around her and held her close, comforting her with Spirit and with touch. "They will let us go soon," she whispered. "Raamo won't let them keep us here much longer."

Before Teera could answer, there was the sound of footsteps just outside the door, and the Kindar serving man, Pino, entered, carrying a tray with food and drink. Pomma sighed with relief. Now Teera would not cry, at least not for a while. The coming of the time for food-taking was still a great comfort to Teera.

"And what games have you been playing today?" Pino asked, as he placed the tray on the tendril table and removed the plates of sliced pan-fruit and nutcake, bowls of spiced mushrooms and goblets of honeyed fruit juices.

"No games," Pomma said. "We haven't played any games today. We haven't felt like playing."

Pino D'erl returned to the heavy, tightly woven tendril door, but he did not open it, at least, not at once. Instead he waited, leaning against the doorframe, and watched the children. They were eating now, two small girl children, one pale-haired and so delicately made as to seem half bird or butterfly. The other, more sturdily built with thick dark hair and a face that seemed to glow with rich, dark colors.

They were beautiful, Pino thought, but then many children were beautiful. But these two were unusual in other ways.

There was the fact, of course, that they had been brought here secretly by the master, D'ol Regle, and that their presence was not to be spoken of. The master had made that very clear. Pino was not to speak to anyone of the children—at any time—for any reason. And Pino had spoken to no one, just as he had promised.

Everyday he had prepared their food just as he had

been told to do; and sometimes he had stood outside the door and watched them for a time before he entered. He had stood there and watched them playing; and it was then that he knew that they were very, very unusual.

Watching them, there had been times when his breath forgot to come and go for amazement, and his heart pounded as it did when he dreamed of being chased by the Pash-shan.

He would have been very glad to discuss them with someone who might be able to explain, and thus relieve his fear that he had lost his wits or that his eyes no longer saw things truly. But he had promised, so he spoke to no one, not even to D'ol Regle himself.

Thus musing, Pino leaned in the doorway until suddenly one of the children, the dark one, noticed him and raised a hand in his direction. Perhaps it was only the start of a greeting, but Pino was frightened; and before the small hand could point directly at him, he slipped away. Closing the door behind him, he slid the heavy bars into place and hurried on about his business.

If the days since the abduction had seemed long and painful to Teera and Pomma, they had seemed at least as long to Raamo and D'ol Falla. Burdened with the knowledge of the children's captivity and uncertain about the return of Genaa and Neric—and still undecided concerning what should be done in the face of the threat made by D'ol Regle and the Geets-kel—they lived each hour in increasing anxiety.

Each day Raamo continued to follow the schedule of the novice Ol-zhaan, attending an endless series of classes and ceremonies. The early hours of each morning still found him in the palace of the Vine-priest, and now he also came again in the evening. Each night after the food-taking in the Hall of Novices had been completed, he returned to wait and watch for the arrival of Neric and Genaa with the Verban, Hiro D'anhk. Before his departure, Neric had said that, on their return, they would approach the Temple Grove through the outer forest and wait in the outskirts of the grove until rain and darkness made it possible for them to reach the Vine Palace without being seen. So Raamo returned, every evening to wait with D'ol Falla until the mid-hours of the night; and while they waited, they spoke of the future and what it might bring.

They spoke of what Neric and Genaa might decide when they heard of the threat, and of what solutions might be offered. They spoke with hope of Hiro D'anhk, and of how, during his days as director of the Academy, he had been noted for his wisdom. And more and more often, D'ol Falla spoke of her own hope that Raamo would find an answer in foretelling.

In the days since the kidnapping of the children, D'ol Falla had spent many hours in the chamber of the Forgotten among the ancient books and records. There she had carefully noted every mention made of the Spirit-gift of foretelling. The references were few and brief, since the gift of foretelling had been rare, even in the early days. The greatest among the foretellers had never established and recorded a prescribed ritual, as had many who were gifted in other ways. But what little was recorded, D'ol Falla carefully copied and then repeated to Raamo during the long hours of their vigil.

Under the guidance of D'ol Falla, Raamo fasted and spent long hours in meditation. He learned the ancient chants attributed to the foretellers of the past. But all with little result.

It was on the seventh night after the taking of the children that D'ol Falla, once more, began to speak to Raamo concerning her hope for a foretelling.

"But I have felt so certain that you have the gift," D'ol Falla told Raamo. "And you have said, yourself, that you foresaw the healing of your sister. You saw that she would be cured when a robed figure with small dark hands reached out to her. And then after the coming of the child, Teera, who is small and dark, the foretelling came true. Surely there is a chance that you could summon the Spirit-force once more, when Pomma is again in great danger. Surely you can find the answer."

Raamo smiled sadly. "The answer," he said. "What is the answer?" Covering his face with his hands, he began to sway to and fro, and after a moment D'ol Falla could hear that he was humming softly to himself.

D'ol Falla sighed and fell into a deep silence, and it was into that silence that the sound came—the sound of many footsteps in the darkened entryway. Shadowy figures crossed the dimly lit reception hall, and a moment later the soft rays of the honey lamp fell on their faces. It was Neric and Genaa and the exiled Hiro D'anhk. Behind them came two strangers, a man and a woman dressed in the close fitting fur garments of Erda. The waiting was over. The travelers had returned.

The Joy of reunion, of adventurers safely home from a dangerous and unprecedented journey, was great—but very brief. There was the truth to be told. The terrible truth of the children stolen and held hostage, and the threats of D'ol Regle and the Geets-kel. Most painful of all was the telling of Herd and Kanna Eld, who had faced the dangers of the journey in good spirits, strengthened by their hope of an early reunion with their child. They came only to learn that she was held captive, and lay under threat of death. The telling had to be repeated many times and in many different ways before the Elds were able to grasp and understand its awful meaning.

At last Herd Eld said, "You tell us, then, that this D'ol Regle, this Geets-kel, has in his possession a weapon capable of causing the deaths of many people in an instant, and that he has said that he would take the lives of Teera and the sister of Raamo if we set about the freeing of the Erdlings, or if we even so much as tell the Kindar the truth concerning what lies below the Root and the true nature of the Pash-shan?"

"Yes," Raamo said. "It is unbelievable to me, even now, but it is true."

Turning abruptly, Herd walked away into the shadows, and Kanna followed. In was many minutes before they returned. When they, at last, came back into the lamp light, the dusky gold of their Erdling skin seemed to have paled and grayed, and their eyes were wet with tears. It was Kanna who spoke first.

"We have spoken together of this thing, and we have come to a decision. We cannot save Teera at the expense of all the people of Erda. The Erdlings are starving, and we were sent here as their representatives. We have no right to barter away the lives of hundreds to save the life of one. Even though the one is of our own flesh."

It was D'ol Falla who spoke at last, after the long silence that followed the words of Kanna. "Truly, the Erdlings are well represented in Green-sky," she said. "But you must know that your sacrifice may be for nothing. If D'ol Regle is capable of killing the two children to save the power of the Ol-zhaan, he is surely capable of killing all those who oppose him. And in the tool of violence, he undoubtedly has the means to do it. I have never seen it used, but I have read descriptions of its terrible effects. It was once used to kill multitudes, and there are in all Green-sky only we seven and the two children who know the truth. And if we die, the truth dies with us."

It was Hiro D'anhk who spoke next. "It seems difficult, almost impossible, to believe that there are many, even among the Geets-kel, who would agree to such evil. In the days when I lived in Orbora as director of the Academy, I often worked with the Ol-zhaan. Can you tell me, D'ol Falla, which Ol-zhaan are among the Geets-kel?"

"There are sixteen, besides myself. Among them are D'ol Wassou, D'ol Birta, D'ol Fanta, D'ol Praavo, D'ol Vesle—"

When the sixteen were named, Hiro shook his head slowly. "I have known nearly all of them well. They were not all as wise and noble as we were taught to believe, but they were—human, and for the most part, I think, well meaning. I cannot believe that they would agree to this—to this atrocity. If we should go to them; if we appear before this Council of the Geets-kel, to which D'ol Regle has summoned us, and if we tell them about the plight of the Erdlings; if they see Kanna and Herd and Teera, standing before them as fellow beings and not as dim and threatening shadows, surely they will see that the Kindar must be told the truth and the Erdlings freed, whatever the changes and dangers that may follow."

"I don't know," D'ol Falla said. "I have asked myself that question over and over, and at times my answer has been the same as yours—that when the time came, and the decision had to be made, finally and irrevocably, that the Geets-kel could not bring themselves to choose such evil. But at other times I am not sure. I have read many of the ancient histories of the days before the Flight, and in that reading I have learned that is almost easier for humans to give up their own lives, and those of their children, than to willingly relinquish privilege and power. I truly cannot say what they will do."

"Perhaps it would be best not to wait to find out," Genaa said. "I know that you, D'ol Falla and Raamo, have promised that you would do nothing until you have appeared before the Geets-kel, but Neric and I have not promised. Nor have my father and the Elds. If we should go now to the city and seek out the leaders of the Kindar, the grundmasters and the learned men of the Academy, and tell them, the truth will spread so quickly that D'ol Regle will not be able to kill all who know it. I know that it would be far better and safer if the Kindar could be prepared more gradually, but it seems now that they must learn at once, or not at all."

"I agree," Neric said quickly. He turned to Hiro and the Elds for their approval, but even as he did so, he was already in motion towards the entry way.

"Wait, Neric," Raamo spoke urgently. "You will not be able to reach the city."

"What do you mean?" Neric asked.

"They are watching. For several nights now when I have come to the palace to wait with D'ol Falla, I have seen them." Turning to D'ol Falla he said, "I did not tell you because there was nothing we could do, and I did not want to burden you further. But I am quite certain. They wait and watch from the branch ends and

Vine clusters around the palace."

"But who? Who are they?"

"I'm not sure. I have not seen their faces. I think that they may be Kindar in the service of D'ol Regle. Or they may be Geets-kel."

The stunned silence lasted only a moment. Then Neric spoke. "How many of them are there? There are six of us here who are strong enough to—"

He stopped there. His face was flushed and twisted with a wild excitement, and his eyes were fixed and rimmed with white. His glance burned across the faces around him. Striding past them, he approached a pedestal that supported a carving of a paraso bird in flight. Seizing the carving, he swung it from side to side with great force, then tossing it aside he grasped the pedestal itself. Holding it before him with both hands, he returned to the others.

"Will you come with me?" he said, and it seemed to Raamo that it was not Neric's voice that spoke. And though they stood face-to-face, staring into each other's eyes, Raamo could awaken not the slightest echo of Spirit-force.

Putting his hands over the fists on the pedestal, Raamo said, "I will go with you but not like this. I will go with you only if you go with open hands."

Neric frowned and raised the pedestal higher above his head, pulling free from Raamo's grasp.

"Stand aside," Neric said, but Raamo continued to stand before him. The heavy pedestal jerked up and back, and D'ol Falla cried out sharply.

At that moment the sound of trampling feet came from the entryway, and three figures moved swiftly forward across the huge chamber. Two of the three wore hooded shubas, and in the dim light it was not possible to distinguish their features, but the third's large and ponderous shape was unmistakably that of the novice-master. As he came closer it was possible to see the familiar face, full and hearty and unchanged in shape and line, but somehow strangely altered—as if a hardening had set in, turning the living tissues into a stony mask. And before him, grasped in both his hands, there was a heavy triangular object with a wide blunt snout.

"The Geets-kel are waiting," D'ol Regle said.

CHAPTER TWENTY

Deep in the leaf-grown far-heights of the Temple Grove, the secret meeting chamber of the Geets-kel hung suspended amid clustering grundleaf and heavy screens of Vine. A long narrow table ran down its length to end at a raised platform, on which stood another smaller table. Seated around the long, lower table, the Geets-kel were, as D'ol Regle had said, waiting.

Mounting the platform with his seven prisoners, D'ol Regle directed them to stand to his left, against the wall, while he seated himself at the small table. Placing the tool of violence carefully on the table before him, he clapped his hands sharply. A large hooded figure entered from a door at the rear of the platform, leading two others, much smaller but also shrouded from view. The hoods that covered the faces of the two small figures made it impossible for them to see, so they were forced to walk slowly, shuffling their feet. When they had been led to the opposite side of the platform, they were bound in place by silken cords, which were passed around their waists and then secured to the grillwork of the wall behind them. The large figure then removed their hoods and retired through the door by which he had come.

Disheveled and tearful, Pomma and Teera blinked and squinted in the sudden light. At the sight of them, a sudden hush fell over the chamber. At the long lower table the men and women of the Geets-kel sat like carved statues, while on the platform the utter silence was broken only by Kanna's soft sobbing gasp. Then Teera turned, and looking past D'ol Regle, she saw for the first time the group of people standing against the opposite wall. Suddenly her tear-stained face was transformed, and holding out both arms she struggled against the bonds that encircled her waist.

At Teera's cry of "Mother," Kanna started forward, but D'ol Regle motioned her back with one hand while the other reached out to touch the weapon that lay on the table before him. She paused only for a moment and would have again moved forward, had not Herd and Neric reached out to hold her back.

Silence again descended, but to Raamo it was a silence that screamed of fear and confusion. The pain of it quickly became unbearable, and for a moment he shut his eyes, trying to shut it out, but it was useless. The turmoil came through to him as if distilled from every breath of air. He struggled against it, fighting to keep his composure, until a sudden harsh grating noise reached through the silent voices of pain, and his eyes flew open.

D'ol Regle had risen suddenly, and it had been the scrape of chair legs that had echoed so harshly in the silent chamber. As all eyes turned to the novice-master, he began to speak.

"Honored members of the Geets-kel," he said. "We are met today to confront the greatest danger, the greatest threat to Peace and Joy, in all the history of Green-sky. And because of this danger we must make a decision, the most difficult and painful decision ever demanded of us, or of any others among the Ol-zhaan in our long history. There are, of course, only two possible alternatives.

"We may decide to release these persons who stand before you on this platform and concede to their demands. If this should be our decision, we must then share the responsibility for the release of the Pash-shan into Green-sky, and for the final and unalterable loss of the innocence and faith that have for so long protected the Kindar from the evils that destroyed our ancestors. Therefore we must consider carefully just what the risks of such a course of action would be.

"We must consider the difficulties and dangers that might arise when the power of the sacred Root of D'ol Wissen has lost its meaning, and the dark hordes of the Pash-shan are free to pour forth into the cities of the Kindar. Consider that, while these Erdlings, as they have named themselves, are in truth not inhuman monsters, they are in fact, far, far removed from the Kindar in many important ways. Consider the fact that they are, and undoubtedly will remain, flesheaters—in a land where the taking of life for any reason has always been unthinkable. Consider the fact that the Erdlings are, for the most part, descendents of those who were banished from Green-sky because of their inability to control the force of their emotions and channel them into expressions of Love and Joy. Consider well this meeting. This meeting of these children of earth and fire—accustomed to the uncontrolled expression of every instinct and emotion—with the Kindar—whose heritage is light and air, innocence and faith, mind and Spirit. What would come of such a meeting, fellow Geets-kel? What *could* come of it?"

As the rich, full voice of D'ol Regle rolled forth, the men and women of the Geets-kel sat in utter silence, their faces blank and impassive. The turmoil of thought and feeling that Raamo had pensed so strongly at the first sight of the captive children was now gone, or carefully hidden by mind-blocking. Staring at the masklike faces, Raamo found it impossible to read the thoughts and feelings that lay behind them.

"And there is yet more to consider," D'ol Regle went on. "We must not forget that if the Kindar learn the true nature of the Pash-shan, they must also learn how and why they were first imprisoned below the Root. And thus they must be told the full truth concerning their own terrible history and the awful fate of their ancestral planet. They will therefore be burdened not only with the knowledge of their own heritage of violence and destruction, but also with the sudden realization that we, the Ol-zhaan, have withheld the truth and led them to believe in things that were not true. Thus, along with their innocence they will lose their faith; and the invasion of the Pash-shan will find them in a state of complete chaos and demoralization."

D'ol Regle paused, and turning away from the Geets-kel, he looked from side to side. First at the two children who now sagged limply in their bonds, clinging together for comfort, their faces crumpled with fear and confusion. He turned next to stare for a long time at his adult captives, at Raamo and Genaa and Neric, at the two Erdlings, at Hiro D'anhk, and at D'ol Falla. And as he stared, the Geets-kel stared also.

Blank-faced and shallow-eyed, the Geets-kel looked at

the three youthful Ol-zhaan, two of whom were still in the first year of their novitiate, wondering, perhaps, what youthful arrogance had driven these three to challenge the customs and traditions of their elders. They stared at the fur-clad figures, the two Erdlings, tawny-skinned, smeared with earth and tears, inhumanly alien in their tight, soft furs and gleaming metal baubles. And at the Verban, the banished one, the brilliant Kindar leader whose compulsive curiosity and un-Kindarlike suspicions had necessitated his banishment to a life of exile. And perhaps they stared longest of all at D'ol Falla—their own D'ol Falla, who for so many years had been revered and honored above all others, and who now stood with this handful of rebels whose very existence threatened everything tried and tested, comfortable and secure. To their eyes D'ol Falla, herself, would seem changed, perhaps. Stripped of her familiar regal dignity, which had always given her a stature that had nothing to do with her actual size, she would seem shrunken, reduced to childlike dimensions. But at the same time, the unique quality of her presence would, perhaps, seem more pronounced than ever—her green eyes alight with a strange new fire. So the Geets-kel stared blank-eyed from behind careful barriers of mind-force, and it was impossible to tell what they might be thinking.

But now D'ol Regle was speaking again. "The other alternative," he was saying. "The only other alternative, would be to make it impossible for these nine individuals to reach either the Kindar, to contaminate them with evil knowledge, or the lower regions, to carry the knowledge of the secret opening in the Root to the Pash-shan. This could be done for the present by shutting them away inside the chamber of the Forgotten until more suitable quarters could be prepared to hold them. It would be possible to construct chambers that would be—"

"A prison." The voice came from the lower table, and D'ol Regle turned his gaze to the Ol-zhaan, D'ol Birta. "Yet another prison?" she said.

"You are right, D'ol Birta," D'ol Regle said. "Such was the term used on the ancestral planet. But I was about to say that it would be possible to construct chambers that would be comfortable and equipped with every necessity, but from which there would be no means of exit. Thus the danger that threatens Green-sky could be averted, and the threat contained. The people of Green-sky, Kindar and Ol-zhaan alike, could continue to live in the Peace and Love and Joy proclaimed by D'ol Nesh-om in the days of the Flight."

D'ol Regle's voice had risen until it rolled forth rich and full, filling the secret chamber with a rhythmic and hypnotic force, and now it dropped suddenly to a compelling whisper.

"These are the choices, fellow Geets-kel. On the one hand change and chaos, danger and despair, and on the other the preservation of all our sacred traditions and values, by the simple expediency of shutting away a handful of dangerous troublemakers. What is your choice, fellow Geets-kel?"

For a moment there was silence. Among the sixteen men and women of the Geets-kel no one moved or spoke, until at last the old Vine-priest, D'ol Wassou, rose to his feet. "Let us hear D'ol Falla," he said. "Let us hear what D'ol Falla has to say of these matters."

Shaking his head, D'ol Regle said, "I think it unnecessary to—" But the approving murmur and nodding of heads among the Geets-kel made it apparent that there were others who agreed with D'ol Wassou. Turning to D'ol Falla he said, "Very well then. What would you say to D'ol Wassou, D'ol Falla, and to all who wish to know why you decided upon the strange and dangerous course that you and these others have taken?"

For a moment D'ol Falla seemed to hesitate; and when at last she stepped forward, her movements were trembling and unsure. Her voice, always husky and wavering, was almost unintelligible as she began to speak. "You must know, D'ol Wassou, and all of you who have known me for so long, why I have decided as I have. My goal is now, as it has always been, the happiness and well-being of the Kindar and the faithful observance of the sacred Oath of the Spirit proclaimed to us by Nesh-om. But I have seen how those goals could never be reached by the paths we have been following. This new path has not been easy for me, and I know it would not be easy for any—not for Kindar, nor Erdling, nor Ol-zhaan. But there is a chance it may succeed. It is only a chance, but to return to the temporary security of the old ways would give us not even that. To return to the separation of the Kindar and the Pash-shan is to return to the ancient evil of separation and loss: the loss of intensity of feeling that comes from separation—of people from people, body from Spirit, thought from feeling; and to that which has so long been happening in Green-sky before our eyes, the slow death of the Spirit-skills, apathy and illness; and finally to the very thing we have most wished to avoid—to violence—to the violence that erupts when the instinct to live fully and intensely is denied, and is at last sought for in desperation, through killing and dying."

For a moment Raamo felt certain that they had won.

D'ol Falla had said it so clearly and completely, surely the others would understand and agree. But then he saw that the faces of the Geets-kel were still blank and empty and there was no understanding in their eyes. Could it be that it had sounded so perfect because he had heard more than words, and the Geets-kel had heard much less?

Clearing his throat confidently, D'ol Regle began to speak again. "It is sadly apparent that our honored colleague has, due to her great age, become irrational. It is obviously irrational to blame the loss of the ability to pense and kiniport on the banishment of the Pash-shan. And it surely is irrational to ask us to trade our present security for almost certain destruction. And not only our own destruction, although it is true that it is certainly we, the Ol-zhaan, who will be placed in the greatest danger. Therefore give me your approval, and I will immediately escort these rebels, renegades and aliens to the chamber of the Forgotten, which has already been prepared for their arrival." As he spoke, D'ol Regle turned towards the table, and for a moment he rested his hand lightly on the weapon that lay there. As if drawn by an irresistible force, every eye in the meeting chamber turned towards the weapon and lingered, as if unable to break away. On the far side of the platform, Teera and Pomma stared at it too, turned to stare wide-eyed at each other, and looked again at the strange object on the table.

Then D'ol Wassou spoke again from the lower table. "And what of your oath, D'ol Regle? What of the Oath of Nesh-om, by which you swore to lift your hand to no one, except to offer Love and Joy?"

Impatiently, D'ol Regle turned once more to face the lower table. Stepping forward, he stared at D'ol Wassou for a long moment before he answered. "I offer no violence," he said at last. "I offer these rebels who have so seriously threatened our well-being only a comfortable and well-cared-for detainment—unless they will not have it so."

"I will not have it so!" It was Neric who shouted, in a voice that throbbed with uncontrolled emotion. Stepping away from the other prisoners, he stood alone near the edge of the platform, facing D'ol Regle. "I will not have it so," he said again, and this time his voice was calmer and even more frightening. "I will not go with you. The others may decide for themselves; but as for me, you must release me or destroy me."

For a moment the two men stared at each other—the one lean and young, visibly trembling and yet terrible in his supreme certainty—the other stately and imperious and no less rigidly certain of his righteousness. D'ol Regle was turning slowly towards the weapon when suddenly D'ol Falla cried out.

"Wait! Stop!" she cried. "This is not the answer. This has never been the answer."

D'ol Falla's voice, usually so slight and rasping, had, for one moment been loud and clear, but now it faded to a weak whisper. "There is another way—another answer. There must be." Turning to Raamo, she reached out to him pleadingly. "Raamo. The answer. What is it?" Grasping his arm, she pulled him forward to stand beside her, between Neric and D'ol Regle.

Staring into the green eyes, caught up in the intensity of her faith in him, Raamo was swept by a sudden feeling of confidence. Surely now, when it was so desperately needed, it would come to him—the answer that D'ol Falla felt so certain he was meant to find.

Closing his mind to all else, he concentrated every

particle of his being and sent his Spirit-force out into the shadows of the unknown, seeking and listening, but no words came to him, nor any images. Instead it came again with maddening insistence, the hauntingly irregular melody of the "Answer Song." He fought against it, trying to shut it out, to reach past it—but to no avail.

When he could hope no longer, he opened his eyes. D'ol Falla was still regarding him pleadingly. Turning away, he looked towards the Geets-kel. Looking down at their upturned faces, it seemed to Raamo that the Geets-kel, too, were expecting a foretelling—depending on him for an answer.

Holding out his hands in a gesture of helplessness, he shook his head sadly. And then, because he had no other message, and because the song, the children's nonsense song, still echoed in his mind, he began to sing:

What is the answer?
When will it come?
When the day is danced and sung,
And night is sweet and softly swung,
And all between becomes among,
And they are we and old is young,
And earth is sky,
And all is one.
Then will the answer come,
Then will it come to be,
Then it will be.

He sang sadly, with his eyes closed against the tears of despair, and his voice fell soft but clear into a deep stillness. He sang it through to the end, and as the last words faded, there was a gasp, and then a low swelling moan, which seemed to come from many throats.

For a moment Raamo thought they moaned for him—for the childish foolishness of his response to their entreaty. But only for a moment, because then he was suddenly aware of the great flowing Spirit-power that he had felt once before—in the palace of D'ol Regle. "Uniforce," a voice breathed. "It is uniforce." Opening his eyes, Raamo saw that the Geets-kel were staring as if in awe, and then rising, one by one, to extend their arms in the Kindar gesture of reverence and respect.

Turning, Raamo looked past D'ol Regle—a D'ol Regle whose majectic bulk seemed strangely shrunken and whose rigid calm had been replaced by what seemed to be a bewilderment that was quickly crumbling into abject fear.

Beyond the trembling mass of the novice-master were the children, Pomma and Teera, still bound and standing against the far wall. But they were not as they had been before. They now stood erect, their arms stretched out before them, their small faces transformed—alight with a deep, still radiance. Their hands, with fingers widespread, reached out towards the center of the platform, to something that was moving slowly towards them through the air.

Airborne, turning slowly in space, the ancient artifact of violence seemed also to be strangely transformed. Relieved of its harsh and heavy nature and rendered airy and unreal, it drifted slowly towards the children and then sank gently to the floor before their feet.

For a moment they stared down at it, their faces still and intent; and then, turning slowly, they looked at each other. For a fleeting instant Teera's full lips curved in a smile that was mischievously triumphant, and Pomma's eyes danced in answer. Then, solemnly, they turned to face the others—and the results of the game they had taught each other how to play.